Fatal Homecoming
Stacey Weeks

P

Write Integrity Press

Fatal Homecoming
© 2018 Stacey Weeks

ISBN-13: 978-1-944120-76-4

Scripture quotations are from The ESV® Bible (The Holy Bible, English Standard Version®), copyright © 2001 by Crossway, a publishing ministry of Good News Publishers. Used by permission. All rights reserved.

Published by Write Integrity Press
PO Box 702852
Dallas, TX 75370
Find out more about the author, **Stacey Weeks,**
at her website: **www. staceyweeks.com**
or on her author page at **www.WriteIntegrity.com**.

Printed in the United States of America.

Contents

Fatal Homecoming

Dedication

Writing is a dream I never really thought was possible during a season of life that holds full-time ministry responsibilities and homeschooling my children. The time my family gives me to write is only one of the many ways they show me that they love me.

Thank you, Kate, Jon, and Nick.
You are a blessing from God, and I love every minute of being your mom. I love how you give me story ideas when I am stuck, how you listen to my plots and laugh at all the right times.

Thank you, Kevin.
You never complain about the hours I spend on the computer as the story comes together. You never tire of listening to my plot threads, and brainstorming misdirects and endings. I love that you give me the freedom to follow my passion. This may seem like a small thing to some people, but they are enormous acts of love to me. I love you.

Chapter 1

Jessica Berns eased open the front door of her old family home, now her brother's house. It creaked on its hinges like it did when she was young, shooting memories through her mind that she'd rather forget. Her chest tightened as she set down her suitcase. She wiped her damp hands on her denim pants and stamped the snow from her boots.

"Hello?" She flicked the light switch in the entryway with no luck. She toggled it up and down, and an eeriness tightened the back of her neck. What were the odds that the college-aged kids stirring up trouble outside hadn't ventured inside?

She slipped down the hall, trailing a finger along the faded wallpaper her mother had chosen the year before she had died in childbirth. The paper looked every day of its twenty-eight years. Jessie tried the kitchen light switch. Still nothing. The kids outside must have turned everything off at the breaker box. She rummaged through a kitchen drawer for a flashlight and hip-checked it shut when she couldn't find one.

The sensation that something wasn't right increased as she made her way toward the electrical panel in her brother's home office. She ignored the old family photographs lining the walls. Her dad always preferred candid shots. The picture at the end had captured her dad laughing at something. He looked down at her and her brother, Frankie. The top of her head brushed the underside of her Dad's chin, and the corners of his eyes crinkled.

She quickened her step. She didn't have time to reminisce. She needed to get the lights on and activate the electric fence surrounding the property. That would stop the rest of Frankie's dogs from escaping. The vandals would stop once they knew someone was home.

A youthful shriek mingled with the barking that trickled through the wood-framed window at the end of the hall. She pursed her lips. The top right pane had never been replaced. A hairline crack snaked its way across the glass to a memory she'd rather forget. The happy family pictures gracing the hallway didn't tell the whole story. When she and Frankie broke that section of glass, her dad had lost control. That was the first time she understood the severity of their financial situation. Her dad couldn't afford to replace a window.

10

She could almost hear her dad yelling at them. That memory, combined with the escalating sounds of the vandals outside, muted a vicious snarl.

Jessie froze.

A German shepherd lunged against a gate almost double the size of a standard baby gate but flimsy in design.

Forward or backward? She could leave the way she came, but that would almost guarantee her brother's dogs would all escape. But even a few steps forward might put her in snapping distance of the canine.

The dog charged again. The gate groaned.

Please, Lord, let it hold. She scrambled toward the open door leading into the back room. Why wasn't the dog in his kennel?

Five more steps.

He crashed through the gate.

A scream tore from her throat. She spun wildly, toppling over a metal shelving unit. A ceramic pot shattered. Items pinged off her head.

She dashed through a door and slammed it. She pushed her back against it as she tried to catch her breath. Her eyes adjusted to the darkness, and a desk and computer dominated the room. She'd landed in Frankie's office.

The door shook against her as the full weight of the dog hurled against it.

She twisted the lock. This was not good. This was not

good at all. But nothing about her return to Chenaniah River was good. She had vowed she would never come back after the small town turned on her family. She wouldn't be here now except her brother was dead. Her dad was still guilty. And she—

The door shuddered again. How long would a hollow core door hold against the shepherd? She raced around the desk and activated the electric fence, thankful the panel was in this room. She slipped out the back door into the maze of runs and gates that usually prevented Frankie's dogs from getting loose. She ran across the backyard and rounded the back corner of the house. Her fingers, numb from the cold, fumbled with the latch on the last gate that opened into the front yard. She hesitated, sweating inside her winter jacket despite the freezing temperature. Her breath puffed out in a fog. The absence of barking was both reassuring and frightening. Was the dog still in the house? Were Frankie's other animals free?

She slipped on the ice and crashed painfully to her knees. She stood and regained her footing. Her footsteps crunched in the frosted snow.

Snarling shattered the silence.

Jessie broke into a sprint. The car. She only needed to make it to her car. *Please, God!* She dug into her pocket and fumbled with the keyless remote. She stabbed the button. The doors unlocked, and she dove inside.

Her knees throbbed, and her palms were skinned, but she was safe. She drew in her first full breath since the chaos had exploded. It had only been five minutes since she called the police to report someone trespassing on Frankie's property.

A small car with tinted windows, sporting a *bumper sticker*, ripped out of the driveway. A lanky college-aged guy leaned out the window, his shaggy hair whipping in the wind. He had the audacity to wave at her. Seriously? This was all a stunt to bring attention to their cause?

She pounded the steering wheel with her hands. Where were the police?

Frankie had loved his dogs. Now, he was dead. The dogs were loose, and the punks responsible were getting away.

Not if she could help it.

She twisted the ignition key and pressed the gas pedal to the floor. The car shot out of the doublewide driveway and careened onto the road. She had been too young to prevent the disaster that destroyed her family, too far from Chenaniah River to save her brother's life, but she could stop this.

She drove as fast as she dared in the worsening road conditions. Squinting, she leaned forward in her seat. It was getting harder and harder to see, and turning on the wipers only smeared slush across her windshield.

Shaggy leaned out the window and tossed a brick in her path.

She twisted the wheel to the right. The brick ricocheted off the front of the car as a shadow passed in front of her. She hit the brakes.

Thunk. The car stopped, and the momentum lurched her forward, then back.

Shaggy sped away.

A distant siren wailed, and the dash clock changed from 7:05 p.m. to 7:06 p.m., only highlighting the delayed response of local reinforcements. But what did she expect? The police had never proven themselves to be reliable, especially when it came to helping her family. Small towns never changed.

She cut the engine and opened her door to investigate the vehicle damage. Something stirred under her front bumper. She froze. Did she hit a deer? *Please, God, please. Not one of Frankie's dogs!*

Her legs shook. She didn't handle the sight of blood well.

"Are you going to stand there all day or are you going to help me up?" A husky voice wafted out from under her front grill.

Her stomach heaved. "No, no! Please tell me I didn't hit you!"

His legs lay partially under her bumper, and his large

hand spanned his upper left thigh. His light jacket, blue jeans, and button-up shirt wouldn't have provided much protection from the snow accumulating at an alarming rate. He suppressed a grimace.

"I'm sorry! I didn't see you!" She reached for his arm.

"I'm fine, but next time keep your eyes on the road." He brushed off her trembling hands even though a second ago he'd asked for her help. He hoisted himself up. The second he stepped on his sneaker-clad foot he doubled over.

Her arms automatically went out to support his weight. His muscular frame tightened under her fingers. "Do you need an ambulance? I could call an ambulance. Or, if my car's not damaged, I can drive…"

"No time." He shook himself free of her hands. His gaze darted past her to Frankie's house, and he took a wobbly step in that direction.

"Wait. Where are you going? At least let me give you my information so that you know how to get a hold of me." She reached for her purse. Argh. She must have dropped it when she upset the shelving unit in the house.

"I don't need your information. I need to keep moving." He hobbled a few steps away, favoring his right leg and squinting into the darkness behind her. White flakes of snow stuck to his eyebrows.

"I just hit you with my car." She stepped alongside him

and laid a hand on his arm. "I suspect, more than anything, you're in shock. You're not fine, and that sore leg will stiffen overnight. We should report this to the police."

"Listen!" He shrugged off her hand.

"At least let me take you to the doctor and have him look at your leg," she said.

"Listen!" he insisted, raising his hand in a slashing motion.

She dragged her eyes over his broad shoulders, powerful arms, and fit frame. A smudge smeared from his chin to his ear camouflaged most of his face. His uncut brownish blonde hair dusted his collar and covered the tips of his ears, shadowing his features. He seemed strangely familiar, but she wouldn't be able to pick him out of a lineup if her life depended on it.

An angry looking muscle twitched in his jaw.

By the time she met his dark eyes the desire to insist on having her way had dissipated. She was alone in the country with a strange man.

A tall, strong, and angry man.

She took a step backward. "Okay, I'll just go then—"

"Jessie, be quiet!"

The use of her shortened name made her hesitate, and his hand clamped onto her upper arm. His long fingers pressed through her heavy coat and into her flesh.

Her breaths shortened.

A branch snapped in the woods.

He twisted toward the sound, and his shirt lifted near his waist. He had a gun!

Fatal Homecoming

Chapter 2

Jessie's rich chocolaty mass of hair danced around her wide dark eyes. The winter breeze manipulated the shorter strands around her face. Rick's fingers itched to brush them back as he did once when they were teens. But her pallid complexion—and his gut—told him that she'd bolt the minute he let go of her arm, and he didn't know who or what lingered in the woods.

"How do you know my name?" She pulled back as far as she could with his hand clamped onto her.

"I hear something." He tightened his fingers. The tree branches rustled. He tucked her behind him, positioning himself between her and the woods. He squinted through the heavy snowfall into the darkness. Were the shadows swaying branches or something more sinister? He nudged her around the vehicle and opened the back door of her car. "Get in."

She scampered inside. "The police are on their way," her voice wavered.

"I am the police." His frustration thundered as he shut her into the vehicle and pulled his gun from his hip holster. He pointed it down, cocked his head, and listened again. *Please, God, keep her safe.*

He'd seen a lot of things as an undercover Royal Canadian Mounted Police officer that he wished he could forget. Some of the worst happened on cold dark nights like this one. And when the crime involved a woman—he shook his head to clear the image of Sarah, the last woman he'd failed to protect.

Stop thinking. Act.

Nothing but tree branches rustled. But something or someone had been there. His gut never lied.

Chief of Police Conrad Brewer, sped past in a cruiser with animal control right behind him. Rick holstered his weapon. If someone had been there, they were long gone now. He opened the driver's door of Jessie's car. Jessie had pushed herself into the corner of the back seat and pulled her knees to her chest. Her head jerked up as he slid into the front seat. He turned the ignition key that she'd left hanging there and shook his head. The car started without issue.

"I'll drive you back to Frankie's, and a uniformed police officer can take your statement." He adjusted the mirrors.

"If you're the police, where's your car? What were you doing hiding in the trees? I could have killed you." She thrust up her chin.

Good. Jessie had some fight in her. She would need it if his suspicions about Frankie proved true.

Her keychain jingled against his thigh. He met her eyes in the rear-view mirror. "You should have palmed the keys instead of leaving yourself vulnerable. Or at least climbed into the front seat and driven away." Shock must be settling in.

A shudder ran over her frame that, if he guessed right, had nothing to do with the cold. Good. She should be afraid. She'd put herself in a dangerous situation. She had nothing but his word that he was a cop.

He made a three-point turn and headed back toward the house. "I live down the road. I heard the call for police on the radio and recognized the address."

"Where's your uniform?" Her eyes followed his through the mirror.

He chuckled. How could she not remember him?

"What's so funny?"

"Your interrogation is a bit late, don't you think? If I had malicious intentions, you're already in the car."

She blanched.

Maybe he should have waited and pointed that out

21

when she had recovered from the shock. "I'm a detective. I don't wear a uniform." His stomach clenched at the necessary lie.

"Detective? Since when do small towns hire detectives?"

"I've only been with the Chenaniah Police Force a month. I transferred in from another city."

"Don't career moves usually go the other way? From small town to big city?" She shifted her weight in the seat and rubbed her hands up and down her arms. Rick turned up the heat, ignoring her questions. He had jumped at the chance to leave his last assignment where he posed as a city cop. He had been eager to leave behind the incompetent label that hack journalist, Anderson, had slapped on him. Anderson had served him up to the public when the news of Sarah, his informant, hit the media. The night Sarah had called him for help, Rick had prioritized another case involving a young mother and child running from an abusive husband. To protect the vulnerable family, Rick refused to disclose the details to reporters. Sarah had died that night waiting for Rick's help.

Reporters couldn't write about the two lives he had saved if they didn't know about them, so they had reported on the life he'd failed. The mother and child he rescued couldn't speak on his behalf while in the protective care of a women's shelter, so he took the character hits. He wouldn't let them come to his defense and jeopardize their safety while the husband still walked free.

Rick had hoped that when the special investigation had cleared him of any wrongdoing, things would settle down. But being professionally cleared didn't erase the guilty verdict already issued by social media, nor did it clear his conscience.

Then his girlfriend had put the cherry on his mud sundae. She couldn't handle Anderson's scathing articles that challenged Rick's abilities and character, so she dumped him. The Chenaniah River assignment provided him with some much-needed distance and an opportunity to prove to himself and his supervisors that he could still do this job.

And if there were local police ties to a drug ring here, he would find them.

At least that was the plan. But then Frankie turned up dead.

Maybe Anderson was right. Maybe he wasn't cut out to be a cop.

He parked the car in front of the house and bounded out to open Jessie's door for her. "If you're off-duty, why are you here?" Jessie studied him from the back seat. She wasn't a woman who took anything at face value.

"As I said, I live nearby. I thought I could get here faster than the cruiser, and I would have if you hadn't run me over."

"You lurk in the dark, and it's my fault I can't see you?" Color flooded her cheeks, sending his heart into a flip. She'd done a great job growing up.

He chuckled. She had a point. "I'm teasing, Jessie. Relax." He motioned for her to climb out and lead the way into the house.

Her brows drew together as she studied him, straightening to her full height. He stuffed his hands in his pockets and nudged her toward the house with his elbow. He then walked ahead of her, hoping curiosity would force her to follow.

He stuffed down a pang of disappointment that she still didn't recognize him. Had he changed that much? "Frankie told me that you've been traveling the world, writing articles for various magazines." His gut soured at the idea of her working as a reporter. Did she exploit innocent people for ratings, too?

She scampered to catch up. "How do you know me?" The corner of her mouth turned up in the familiar and quirky way that it had when she was young.

"It's me, Jessie. Rick Chandler."

She stopped at the bottom of the porch stairs and narrowed her eyes in squinted concentration. He couldn't blame her. He looked nothing like the kid who was always getting into scrapes with her brother.

Jessie studied him a moment longer then brought her hand up to cover her mouth. "Rick? I'm so glad I ran into you!"

"Literally." He made a face and rotated his shoulder.

"I'm sorry." Her tone held just a hint of a smile. It released some of the pent-up tension he'd carried since he'd heard of her planned return.

"I'm sorry about Frankie," he said.

She nodded, and joy drained from her eyes.

She moved as if she were about to hug him but then seemed to reconsider. She twisted her hands together in front of her. "It's good to see you again. Sorry that I didn't recognize you."

He would have welcomed a hug from her, but he followed her lead and kept his hands in his pockets. "Don't worry about it. Neither of us are the same kids we used to be."

A uniformed man from the Humane Society exited the house. He nodded at Rick and then addressed Jessie. "Are you Miss Berns?"

Jessie nodded.

"The dog is contained. You can search the building now."

Jessie trembled.

Rick stepped closer, wishing for familiarity that would have allowed him to comfort her. She never liked being coddled when she was fifteen. She probably wouldn't like it any better now at—he did some fast calculations—twenty-eight? Twenty-nine?

"What about the other dogs?" Jessie asked. "Did they get out?"

"Some," the animal control officer admitted. "We are heading out to collect them now. I doubt they got too far."

"Thank you."

"The main breaker was off, so the chief flipped it back on. Everything should work now."

"Walk me through what happened tonight." Rick fell into step beside her as Jessie moved through the front door. She hung up her jacket on the hooks by the entry and stepped around a suitcase. Her dark fitted jeans and tailored cotton blazer were suitable for a freelance travel writer, but he remembered her more carefree. The pigtailed girl who trailed after Frankie and him, begging to be included in their foolishness, bore little resemblance to this professional woman.

"I'm not sure what happened. I arrived later than expected. I had hoped for enough time to go through some of Frankie's stuff and get ready for the funeral. When I pulled up to the house, my headlights exposed some kids trying to open the back gate to let the dogs go."

"Kids?"

"Well, not little kids. Student age. Like college or

university."

He nodded. "Where does the back-gate lead?"

"The gate on the outside perimeter opens into the ravine. The ravine backs up to a creek and the creek opens into Chenaniah River."

"Then what happened?"

"I came in the front. I thought I could activate the electric fence so that if the dogs got out, they'd at least stay on the property, but none of the lights worked, and one of the dogs cornered me in the house."

"You didn't know about Max?" Rick found it hard to believe that Frankie never told his sister about Max. Max was the first dog Frankie had trained, and he held a special place in Frankie's heart.

"I knew about him, but he was supposed to be in a kennel. The police officer who called me about Frankie's death said he was locked up at night. Maybe the kids let him out first?"

"But then left him in the house? That doesn't seem to fit. Who did you speak with at the police station?"

"Officer Thorn."

Rick nodded. Gavin Thorn was a bit young and overeager, but he had good potential as an officer. Now that he had married, he'd likely settle down.

Heavy footsteps in the hall preceded Chief Brewer's entrance. "Everything covered here?"

"I'm just getting her statement, sir." He didn't ask why the chief had responded to a petty disturbance call. Conrad Brewer's demeanor didn't invite questions. Ever.

Brewer settled a fierce gaze on Jessie.

She didn't blink.

A crazy part of his heart swelled like it did that day when they were kids, and local officers had questioned them about a prank at the school. Even as she had backhanded tears, she stood her ground.

"And you are?" Brewer asked.

"Jessica Berns." She stepped forward and held out a hand. "I'm Frankie's younger sister. I appreciate the chief of police responding personally to my call. That's more than I expected."

Rick snorted but quickly covered it with a cough. He had been on the job long enough to know the chief didn't go above or beyond duty requirements unless it benefited him in some way.

Brewer accepted Jessie's offered hand. "Happy to help."

"You were telling me about Max," Rick reminded her.

Jessie fixed her attention on Rick. "Max backed me against the wall." She pointed at a family picture that sat askew. She straightened it as they passed, walking down the corridor and pointed to a shelf on its side. "I knocked this over, and it slowed Max down long enough for me to get through the office door. Here are the nail marks from where he jumped against it." She pointed to the scratches on the door then picked up her purse from the floor. Some of the marks cut clean through the hollow door. It wouldn't have offered protection for much longer.

Jessie smiled at Rick, and something deep inside his chest stirred. He quickly doused it. She was a victim. A reporter. His buddy's sister. Nothing more.

Her purse strap slipped from her shoulder, and a clear medicine bottle toppled out. It rolled toward the chief who scooped it up and frowned. "Ms. Berns, you're going to need to come to the station with us."

"Why?" The question popped out before Rick could stop it. There was no reason to drag her into the station over a minor disturbance.

The chief tossed him the pills, and he caught them in one hand.

He turned the bottle over. His gut hardened. These couldn't be Jessie's. He held up the bottle and rattled it. "Why do you have this?"

"What is it?" She reached for it, but he pulled his hand back.

Her eyebrows lifted. "When I toppled the shelves, a bunch of stuff fell on me. It must have dropped into my purse."

Rick narrowed his eyes. Why were the same street

drugs involved in Frankie's death tucked inside her purse? When some old man at Chenaniah Manor Retirement Home had pressed drugs into Frankie's hands, Frankie had called Rick. Frankie knew his addiction history would impact the believability of his statement, but he died before Rick could question him further, and the drugs had vanished... until now.

Chapter 3

Jessie rested her forehead on her folded arms and closed her eyes. She wouldn't be in this mess if she had arrived during the light of day. She got stuck behind some poky farmer's tractor on the single lane road, pulling what she could only guess were the bones of some parade float. All she wanted to do was settle Frankie's estate and find some answers.

At least Rick had afforded her some dignity by allowing her to drive herself to the station instead of tossing her into the back of a cruiser. She'd spent the better part of the last hour praying that God would get her out of this mess. Now, she was just plain tired. She wanted to go home. She wanted a drink of water. She wanted some answers.

The barren room housed a single table with two chairs, bright and unflattering lights, and a huge mirror on one wall. According to the latest crime shows, the mirror was one-way glass, allowing someone to watch her squirm. Maybe Rick.

As if on cue, he walked in the room and closed the door behind him. He had removed his jacket, rolled up his shirtsleeves, and washed the muddy imprint of her bumper off his face. He didn't look like a cop. His disheveled hair fell over his eyes more beach-boy than one of the boys-in-blue. A crazy urge to brush it off his face made her fingers itch. She folded her hands in her lap.

His footsteps echoed in the room as he placed a pitcher of water and two glasses on the table between them and sat down in front of a yellow notepad and pencil. "Tell me again what happened tonight." Rick leaned on his forearms. He looked comfortable on that side of the table, the powerful law-abiding side of the table. Gone was the easy smile. His guardedness suggested that he didn't trust her. It shouldn't bother her, but it did.

She stiffened and pressed her fingertips against her forehead, shading her eyes to hide the pain burning behind them. She'd been happy when she recognized Rick. A nostalgic part of her had welcomed the idea of grieving Frankie with someone who had loved him before addiction had changed him. But like every other man in a position of power over her, Rick let her down. Worse, he hauled her into the police station for questioning like a common criminal. At least she wasn't under arrest. Yet.

He lifted his eyebrows.

After a steadying breath, she launched into a recap of her evening for the umpteenth time. *Lord, give me patience.*

"Was the front door locked when you arrived?"

"Of course, it was," she responded automatically. But wait, was it? "I can't remember for sure. I had my keys out. I put the key into the lock, but I don't recall with certainty whether I actually unlocked the door."

He made a note.

"I went into the kitchen to look for a flashlight because the lights weren't working."

Rick glanced toward the huge mirror.

She wiggled her fingers at whoever listened from the other side. Her reflection waved back.

Rick jerked his attention back to his papers too slow to hide his smile. He scratched down something else on his notepad, probably that she was a bit of a smarty-pants.

"Do you remember the last time I waved through one-way glass?" She tipped her head to the side and studied him. They had been kids, dragged in for toilet-papering the school.

"Yeah." He smiled.

This smile looked more like the boy she remembered, a little cocky and a little too proud of his crazy adventures.

She reached for some water. "You always had my back."
A slosh of water spilled over the rim of the pitcher.

"I still do." He took the pitcher from her trembling hands and filled her glass. He slid the glass halfway to her like he expected her to meet him in the middle.

She hated what his actions implied, but she reached for the glass anyway. "If you're on my side, why are you on the wrong side of the table?"

He blinked. "The best way I can help you is by doing my job."

Her heart hiccupped. He *looked* concerned.

"I'm on your side," he pressed.

They stared at each other. Neither blinking. Neither moving. Like an adult version of chicken.

Jessie finally turned her face away and caught her reflection. Dark purple circled her eyes, accentuated by her pale skin and the harsh lighting. She needed sleep more than she needed to go over the excitement of the night one more time. "So, what's the big plan here? Are you charging me with something?"

Rick's gaze drilled into her profile. "Did you do something illegal?"

She sent him the same look she reserved for deflecting unwelcome male attention. As a travel writer, she never remained in one place long enough to invest in meaningful relationships, so she had learned to master the nonverbal

34

cues that tell a man to back off.

Rick didn't even flinch. He held her gaze.

She puffed out a shuddering breath. She had geared herself up for a night of memories and regret... but not this.

"You look defensive. Do you have a reason to be on guard?" He tapped the end of his pencil against his pad of paper in an annoying rhythm.

"Reason? You need a reason?" she snapped. "How about I come home grieving my brother's death and run into an old friend..." She put air quotes around the word friend. "...and instead of helping me like he is supposed to, as an old friend should, he drags me into the police station like I've done something wrong. But the only thing I did wrong was call the cops to report trespassers." She palmed the tears that finally spilled over. "I should have handled it myself."

His face flushed. "It's never wise to confront intruders alone. Calling the police was the right move."

"A lot of good it did me." She pushed the glass of water away from her. "Nothing has changed here. My family name makes me guilty until proven innocent. Just like always. It's why we left. It's why I never planned to come back."

All the shame she'd felt when her family left Chenaniah River after her ninth-grade year rushed back. The factory that employed half the town, Eastmore

Incorporated, had closed, and it devastated the whole area. Her father had been accused of stealing the pension money. It was never provable in court, so no charges were laid, but the town had already judged him guilty. In a blink, everything changed. Dad's friends were no longer able to retire in comfort, and they turned against him. Dad couldn't even sell the house because no one would do business with him. It sat vacant until Frankie moved into it.

"This isn't about the past." Rick's grip on his pencil tightened, and it sent a muscle rippling up his forearm.

She swallowed and forced his physique from her mind. She leaned across the table and into his space as far as she dared and whispered, "It sure feels like the past. Only this time, you're sitting across from me instead of beside me." She slumped back and folded her arms across her chest.

He leaned into his chair back and raked a hand through his hair, pushing those boyish strands off his face.

She got to him. It made her smile.

"Do you have a problem with me leading the investigation?" he asked.

She did, but for all the wrong reasons. It wasn't Rick's fault that Chief Brewer insisted he bring her in for questioning. If she had been in the chief's position, she'd have questioned her, too. Her problem was rooted in the memories Rick stirred. She'd always wanted him to notice her, to see her as more than Frankie's little sister. Feelings she'd thought had long ago evaporated had resurfaced with a vengeance the second she had recognized him. "It's fine."

Rick bent across the table and invaded Jessie's space in a carbon copy of her previous move. His whispered words rubbed her raw. "I guess we're stuck with each other."

A knock on the door sliced the tension, and Rick left the room.

She sagged into the chair. He definitely noticed her now, but not for the reasons she desired. She no longer cared who watched her through the mirror.

Why did Rick have to look so good? Why couldn't he have gained weight or developed some poor hygiene habit that would repel her? She didn't have the strength to fight a renewed crush on top of everything else, and she certainly didn't have the time for romance. Logic must prevail despite the way her traitorous heart responded.

Rick returned with her winter coat in his arms. "You're free to go."

She snapped to attention. "What? Just like that?"

He grinned, looking as happy as she felt. "Did you want to stay? I could arrange for more questioning."

"No!" She jumped to her feet. "What changed?"

"Our preliminary findings show that the bottle didn't have your fingerprints on it. If you had tucked it into your purse, it would have had prints." He held out her jacket so she could slip her arms into it.

So that's why he snatched the bottle back from her when she tried to look at it. Maybe he was on her side after all. "I wish my word would have been enough for you." She spoke to his reflection in the mirror since he stood behind her.

He adjusted the coat on her shoulders and tightened his lips as he turned her around to face him. The weight of his hands on her shoulders sent a ripple of warmth through her veins.

"That's not fair," he said. "Friend or not, I have to follow the evidence. Evidence always leads to the truth."

"Were Frankie's prints on the bottle?" She stood so close to him that she had to tip her head back to read his expression. Deep down, she didn't want to believe Frankie had relapsed... not when everything had been going so well for him.

"His, mine, and the chief's fingerprints. I'm sorry."

She nodded and bit her lip. She wouldn't cry in front of him.

"Do you have any questions?"

Questions? She had lots of questions but none she was ready to ask. Like why did Frankie establish his business in the town that destroyed their family? Why would God free him from drug addictions only to let him die from an asthma attack? And where were all his inhalers?

"No." She held her head high as Rick held open the door to the interrogation room and motioned for her to go through. She sailed past Chief Brewer, Officer Thorn, and the others hovering just outside the door.

Officer Thorn touched her arm as she passed. "I called a guy who used to work with Frankie. His name is Sam—Sam's Animal Training. He's able to help with the dogs."

Her stiff posture relaxed a bit. She hadn't expected that. "Thank you. That was thoughtful."

She wrapped her fingers around the steel pull on the exterior door just as someone pushed it from the outside. "Oh, sorry—"

"Jessica? Aren't you a sight for sore eyes!" Strong arms pulled her into a quick embrace.

"Steadman?" She hadn't seen her mother's cousin in almost ten years.

He smiled widely, and her eyes welled up. At least someone was happy to see her.

"Good evening, Mayor," Rick said.

Jessie's head swiveled from Rick to Steadman. "Mayor?" Her mouth slackened. A lot had changed in ten years.

"I assumed you knew?" Steadman's smile dimpled his cheek.

She turned back to the chief, now bolstered by the presence of not just family—but powerful family. Maybe she would not have to do this alone? "I'd like to see a copy of the report on my brother's death, please."

Chief Brewer flicked his gaze up to the ceiling and sighed. "I'm sorry, but that's not possible."

"Should I fill out the Municipal Freedom of Information and Protection of Privacy form?"

Steadman chuckled and pressed a hand to the small of Jessie's back. It felt good to know he was standing with her. "I think my cousin is within her rights to request that information, Chief Brewer."

Jessie forced her expression to remain neutral, but her insides tap-danced.

"You can fill out any form you want." The chief's smile didn't quite reach his eyes.

She nodded. "I will."

Steadman scooped up her hands and squeezed them. "Beth and I are so sorry about Frankie. We'd love a chance to hear how you've been. Let me know when you have time. We'll plan a meal."

She nodded.

"I have a meeting with the chief, but we'll catch up soon." Steadman gave her hands a final squeeze and followed the chief into his office. He turned at the last minute. "Oh, I have some of Frankie's photography at my house. I collected his negatives from his darkroom before you arrived so I could have them developed. I hope you don't mind. We're going to feature his work at the Valentine's Diamond Ball and Art Show. It's my way of honoring him."

Her eyes filled at his thoughtful gesture. Frankie had a natural talent for photography. It was nice that Steadman would honor him this way.

He turned and followed the chief into his office.

Jessie waved at Rick as she exited. She just had to get through the next few days. Plan a funeral. Close Frankie's business. Get back to work. Writing for *Travel the World With Us* magazine wasn't the hard-hitting journalism she'd once dreamed of writing, but it was a decent job.

The lamppost she'd parked under offered just enough light. A white paper fluttered under her windshield wiper, nearly buried by the snow. With her luck, she'd probably been ticketed for parking in one of the police station's visitor spaces for too long. The only vehicles left in the visitor lot were hers and a dark gray compact. She squinted at the vehicle as she unfolded the damp paper.

You're not safe in Chenaniah River. Trust no one.

A force from behind slammed her face against the car door. Someone wrenched her arm behind her back and pinned her against her vehicle. Heavy breathing filled her ear. "Go back where you came from. You're not welcome here."

With a final shove, she was free. She stumbled to the

right. Footsteps slapped on the wet pavement as she landed hard on her hands and knees. Arms then encircled her.

"No!" She twisted her body and thrust her head back, connecting with a skull. It was hurt or be hurt. She threw her whole weight into swinging her elbow around.

"It's me!" Rick's breath whooshed out as her elbow connected.

The fight left her, and she crumpled.

"It's okay. I'm here." He released her and squatted in front of her. His eyes roamed over her, checking for injury.

She stilled, but he moved in and out of focus.

"Are you okay?" He tentatively reached out and brushed her hair back from her face.

His fingers hardly grazed her skin, yet heat rose in her neck. Faintheartedness threatened again but for a whole different reason this time.

She blinked rapidly, and the fuzz cleared. Snowflakes clung to his eyelashes and lingered a millisecond before melting. Her old wild crush on him thudded through her chest. She pushed herself up, skimming her fingertips along her sore jawline and licking her lips. She handed him the note still clutched in her hand. "Someone left this on my car."

He helped her sit and then flipped open the folded paper. "You better come back inside."

His frown sent shivers down her spine.

Chapter 4

The next evening, Rick sat on Frankie's couch across from a wood stove and nursed the fire. A soft glow filled the room. With Max at his feet and Jessie puttering around in the kitchen making supper, he could almost pretend this cozy domestic scene was real. Except the fire was for warmth, not romance. And Jessie only invited him to stay for dinner because the surveillance video of the police station parking lot hadn't arrived yet.

They'd spent the day sorting through boxes and papers and memories. Hearing her laugh did good things to his heart. She should be able to enjoy some good memories from her childhood, and he would do whatever he could to remind her that it wasn't all bad.

He had convinced himself he was there as a friend instead of a cop until she uncovered a paper trail of monthly cash deposits of $1500 in Frankie's accounts mixed in with various ancestry documents. The investigator in him took over. He'd get Daniel, the Chenaniah police tech guy, to take a look at them when he examined Frankie's computer. Hopefully, that would shed some light on things.

The ring of Jessie's cell phone broke the quiet.

Rick urged himself from the warm seat and joined her in the kitchen. "Do you recognize the number?"

She shook her head.

"Put it on speaker."

She gave him a look that screamed she didn't like being told what to do, but she turned down the stove under the bubbling soup and pressed the speaker button anyway.

"Hello?"

"This is Sam Bommel, from Sam's Animal Training. I got your number from Officer Gavin Thorn. Is this Jessica Berns?" Sam's voice boomed through the room.

She pulled a kitchen chair out from the chrome-rimmed table and sat down across from Rick. "You can call me Jessie. You're on speakerphone. I'm here with Officer Chandler."

"Frankie and I weren't just competitors. We also worked together. I think I can help you," Sam said.

"Oh?"

"He'd started coming with me to Chenaniah Manor Retirement Home. We brought our dogs there for therapy visits. You'd be surprised how cheery a grumpy old man becomes after playing with a dog for twenty minutes."

Jessie knitted her eyebrows together and tossed Rick a puzzled look.

Rick shrugged his shoulders. He had no clue what Sam was building up to.

"You must be eager to put this place behind you," Sam said.

Ah. Understanding dawned on Rick. Sam wanted the business.

Guilt flashed across Jessie's face. She covered her eyes with her hand and stammered, "I, ahh…"

"Lay off the hard sell, Bommel," Rick cut in. "She's grieving."

Jessie had to know that selling the dogs was necessary. She couldn't keep animals while traveling for the magazine, but that didn't mean he'd let guys like Sam start circling before she was ready.

"Officer Thorn thought you might need some help," Sam's voice trailed off.

Jessie bit her bottom lip.

"I helped Frankie all the time," Rick cut in. "I can help her."

Sam chuckled like he didn't believe it. "The dogs require a lot of attention. More than most people realize."

"I know what the dogs need, and I'm only a minute or two down the road."

There was a long pause. "Okay. But if you ever want to see my dogs in action, Miss Berns, I bring them to Chenaniah Manor every Thursday to interact with the residents. My brother, Derek, owns the place."

"I'll keep that in mind. Thank you." Jessie disconnected.

She avoided Rick's gaze as she stood up, so Rick moved closer and forced eye contact. His stomach churned at the growing bruise of purple coloring her forehead that reminded him that he had been too late to catch the guy who attacked her at the police station.

Stormy emotions raged across her features.

"Until we know what's going on, you shouldn't accept help from strangers."

"But Officer Thorn—"

"I'd like your cell number." Rick rocked back onto his heels and tapped his phone screen.

She rhymed off the digits, and he punched them into his phone. Her cell dinged in her hand.

"That's from me. Add my contact to your phone."

She did. Then she turned away, hurried to the stove, and stirred the soup. She cleared her throat. "Dinner is almost ready."

The way her voice caught made him want to tell her everything about the RCMP and their investigation. Between her father's deception and the questions surrounding Frankie, she deserved honesty from at least one man in her life.

Except he couldn't. He couldn't tell anyone. No one but Rick's RCMP handler, Pete Ryerse knew that Rick's real assignment was to investigate the police department. Theories about drugs, dirty cops, and this small town had reached the provincial level. Pete had warned Rick to trust no one on the force, not even the chief.

Ryerse had warned him it would be hard to withhold the truth from people he knew. He called it, *putting aside what is good for what is best.* Pete's advice was easier to accept before Jessie rolled back into his life. Would Jessie see his lies of omission as being necessary to obtain the greater good? Or would she run like his old girlfriend the minute things got hard?

Headlights beamed across the room, and a car pulled up in front of the house. Max stood and looked at Rick.

"Stay," he commanded. Rick had spent much of the day getting Jessie used to Max, thankful for the time he had spent with Frankie and the dog. He'd feel a whole lot better about her being in this big farmhouse alone if she kept Max around.

Heavy footsteps tromped onto the porch. Rick urged Jessie to stay behind him as he peeked out the side window. Catching the site of police tech, he released his breath and opened the door.

"As promised." Daniel produced the thumb drive containing video footage from the parking lot.

"See what you can find on here." Rick exchanged it for Frankie's laptop.

"Will do." Daniel nodded.

Jessie retreated to the sofa and tugged an afghan over her legs. The headlights shone across the room as Daniel's vehicle pulled away. She powered up her laptop and handed it to Rick. He plugged in the thumb drive.

She leaned closer, her hair swinging forward and brushing Rick's arm. Her lilac scent tickled his nose like sweet heaven on a spring day and made the air heavy. Almost too heavy. He cleared his throat. They pressed their heads together and watched in fast-forward until there was movement by her car.

"That's it. That's my car," she whispered.

Rick clicked the touchpad a few times, and the image zoomed in as a hunched man in a blue hooded jacket popped a note under her windshield wiper.

"Come on, turn around." She tapped her fingers on her thigh. "He just needs to turn a little bit."

The man scurried away.

"That doesn't help," Jessie moaned.

"I told you we reviewed it yesterday. It didn't have anything helpful."

"I hoped I'd see something you missed."

"There's more." Rick fast-forwarded the recording until Jessie had left the station.

She stiffened beside him as they watched a man dressed entirely in black approach her from behind and shove her against the car. The man never turned toward the camera. Rick's throat closed up as the lowlife escaped.

She bolted upright in her seat. "That's not the same guy!"

He was impressed she noticed. The second man was taller and thinner. His build was different, lanky even.

"That wasn't what I had expected at all." She sat back against the sofa cushions. "Are the note writer and the attacker working together, or is it a strange coincidence that both accosted me on the same night?"

"We're not sure." Her detachment impressed him. He had expected that watching her attack on film would stir feelings of helplessness.

Jessie heaved herself off the couch and returned to the stove. "I was hoping the video would provide some answers."

Rick followed her, watching as she ladled soup into bowls. "Real police work isn't like television. Things don't come together in sixty minutes or less." He set the laptop on the kitchen table and clicked a few buttons, zooming in on the best partial profile picture of the guy leaving the note, cropping it to a headshot. He twisted the laptop so she could see the screen. The blowing snow didn't help the image, but it was the best lead they had. "We've already logged the description of this guy but got nowhere on the BOLO. Do you recognize him?"

She placed the soup bowls next to the spoons on the kitchen table and studied the man. "It's hard to say. I can't see enough to know for sure." Her shoulders hunched forward.

Rick zoomed back out to full-size image.

"Wait, that car!" She pointed at the vehicle parked near hers.

He squinted at the screen. "What about it?"

"It kind of looks like the one those coeds were driving when they let out the dogs."

"I thought you didn't remember the make of the car they drove?"

"I don't, but it was dark colored and sort of looked like that." She crinkled her nose. "Plus, a similar looking one might have been outside the house earlier today."

"Why didn't you say something?" He hurried to the window.

"It was idling at the side of the road. The next time I looked, it was gone. I didn't put it all together until now."

Rick returned to Jessie's computer and clicked a few more buttons. No angle provided a readable view of the license plate. He pocketed the thumb drive and flipped the laptop closed.

She gripped the chair back. "I return to bury my brother and stumble onto street drugs, odd bank deposits, and being attacked in the police parking lot. This doesn't make sense."

Could he answer truthfully without piquing her journalistic interest? If he didn't tell her about Pete's RCMP investigation, and she found out on her own, she'd only mistrust the police more. But if he told her, it could cost him his job.

"What do you recall about Frankie's habits with his inhalers?" He pulled out a chair and sat down at the table. He motioned for her to sit down across from him.

"When he was younger, and the years he was in trouble, he was reckless. But this last year everything had changed. He'd become quite responsible."

Rick nodded. "Frankie was always in reach of an inhaler. He kept spares in desk drawers, glove compartments, everywhere."

She heard what he wasn't saying. "There were no inhalers in the drawer when I looked for the flashlight the night I arrived. He always has extras stashed around the house just like I always carry an EpiPen for my coconut allergy. Where were his inhalers when he died?"

"That's the problem. There weren't any. When I told the police, they thought I was too close to be objective."

Her face flushed, and she fisted her hands. "If they won't investigate properly, I will."

"Calm down, Nancy Drew. I'm on it."

She eyed him. "You'll tell me everything?"

"Of course." *When I can.*

She pushed her chair back and returned to the sink, leaving her soup untouched. Dishes rattled in the soapy water. She tucked her chin into her chest, but she couldn't hide the tears that dripped from her jawline.

"Jessie?" He swallowed a lump in his throat and approached from behind. He wanted to reach out to touch her shoulder, but would she welcome it?

She spun around. He braced himself to absorb her weight, but she drew herself up short, fisted her hands in a dishtowel, and rocked back on her heels. "Frankie worked so hard to get clean, to start a new life." She pulled her sleeve over her fist and swiped across her eyes.

Rick jammed his hands into his pockets and gave himself a lecture. Had she flung herself at him, he would have comforted her, but not like a cop and definitely not like a friend of her brother.

"I thought he was doing okay," she sniffled, "that he had overcome his demons." She looked past him out the kitchen window, frowning.

He followed her line of sight. Snow blew across the backyard and drifted into large piles near the kennel doors.

The bright lights of the kitchen made it hard to see anything else in the darkness. "What do you see?"

Max sat up and growled. His hackled raised.

Rick stiffened. Guard dogs don't spook. He shoved Jessie away from the window just as the crack of a gunshot split the air.

Jessie screamed as Rick dove for her. He knocked her to the ground, covering her with his body and unholstering his weapon in one motion.

Splinters of glass blanketed the worn linoleum.

Fatal Homecoming

Chapter 5

Under Rick's watchful eye, the paramedic bandaged Jessie's scrapes. "She'll be fine?" Her fair skin looked even paler against the dark fabric of the sofa where she reclined.

"She doesn't even need stitches." The medic patted Jessie's arm. "All done."

Officer Gavin Thorn shoved the back door open, trekking in snow on his boots. "I found some casings up on the hill." He wiped his feet on the doormat and wiggled an evidence baggie in their direction.

"What kind of weapon?" Rick took the bag and studied the brass.

"Looks like a Remington .22-250 rifle. Pretty common gun around here. A lot of people hunt with them."

Jessie perked. "This is good, right? This will help you find him, right?" She swung her legs around in front of the couch and dropped her slippered feet on the floor. She pushed herself up and nodded at Gavin. "Let me get you a coffee. It's the least I can do."

"You sit." Rick pulled out a kitchen chair for her. "I can make the coffee." He rattled around in the kitchen talking over his shoulder. "Forensic Science can use this to match the weapon, but we have to find it first. Until we do, this doesn't mean much."

"What was your brother into?" Gavin asked.

Rick plunked a coffee in front of Jessie and handed one to Gavin.

Jessie wrapped her hands around the steaming mug and furrowed her brow. "Maybe it has nothing to do with Frankie. Maybe someone is still angry about Dad and the pension money, although I can't imagine anyone trying to kill me for it."

Rick got it. She was grasping at straws, not wanting to believe her brother had fallen back into old habits.

Gavin looked unconvinced. "No one bothered Frankie before, and he had been back for a while."

She bristled. "What are you trying to say?"

Rick repositioned Jessie's chair, so her back was to Gavin and his pitying look. "Things don't add up." He pointed at the wall. "The shooter wasn't aiming to kill."

She puckered her forehead. "How do you know that?"

"He is either a terrible shot, or he was just trying to scare you. The shot was too low." He pointed at the floor where the corner met the wall. "The trajectory is all wrong if he was aiming for you."

She followed his hand gestures with her gaze, but she didn't seem to get it.

"The type of rifle that matches the casing Officer Thorn found has a 300-400-yard range. A good hunter can take down a coyote at that distance. You should have been an easy target."

"So, at best, someone just wants to scare me. At worst, a guy with bad aim failed to kill me. I'm not sure if I feel better or not." She wrapped her arms around her middle.

After another hour or so of statements and police officers milling about, Rick finally closed the door on the last person to leave. He fired off a quick text message to Pete, briefly updating him on the situation. They were supposed to connect so Rick could update him on the drug investigation, but there was no way he'd make their scheduled meet on time. He couldn't leave Jessie with a hole for a window while the gunman was still out there.

His phone beeped. It was Pete. *O.K. C U @ the alt location @ 12 a.m.*

He stuffed his phone into his pocket. That gave him just enough time to get Jessie settled for the night and that window boarded up. Officer Thorn had left and returned with some planks of wood.

Jessie squatted in front of the fire and pensively poked

it with the fire iron. The flames breathed in the fresh oxygen and roared. "What do you think is going on?" she asked.

Rick tilted a board out from where it leaned against the wall and eyeballed the kitchen window, comparing them in lengths. Looked good. "I don't know."

She stood and surveyed the mess left by the police and paramedics. "Do you think Frankie was into something serious?"

Of course, Nancy Drew was theorizing. Instinct would be fight or flight, and he'd never known her to run from anything until the day her dad dragged her out of town in shame. But he couldn't freely speculate, not without jeopardizing his cover. "I didn't see any evidence that he was into anything suspicious."

"But addicts are good at hiding their secrets." She meandered toward the kitchen, scooping up a framed picture of Frankie and her off the end table. It was taken the last summer, before they moved away, before he fell into drugs. "I should have been here for him."

The last thing he needed was Jessie driven by a guilty conscience and digging her heels into the case. If that happened, she'd never leave after the funeral as planned. He needed her to leave—for her safety.

He held a board horizontally against the window then stood it on its end and measured it against the other three planks leaning against the wall. He should have just enough wood. "Can you grab plastic bags or something? We should seal the window first to keep out the wet." There was nothing like a little hard work to snap a person from nostalgia. "If we don't seal it up soon, you'll freeze tonight." The roaring fire couldn't compete with the rapidly dropping evening temperature without the window in place.

She started pulling out random kitchen drawers, chewing her lip. "I know the police searched the house, but could there be more drugs somewhere? Besides the ones that fell into my purse." She slammed a drawer shut.

"Try the bottom one," he suggested.

"Found them!" She victoriously held the plastic bags up.

"Impressive," he said wryly, "considering I told you where to find them."

"You should ask me to find something challenging, like the lost diamond of Chenaniah River." She handed over the bags.

"We spent a lot of hours looking for that gem, didn't we? If you want to break and hunt a diamond, I'm game. We make a pretty good team, and the festival just released this year's clues."

Back in the 1920s, Jessie's great, great, great, great grandparents, a bootlegging millionaire and his wife, lived in Chenaniah River. Legend said her Grandma Maggie dropped a valuable diamond in the snow and it was never found.

"When did Chenaniah River reinvent itself as a tourist destination?" Jessie opened a garbage bag and started to carefully collect the larger pieces of broken glass.

"When Mayor Munroe—I mean, your cousin—won the election, he capitalized on the legend and started the Winter Diamond Festival. The annual hunt was already happening. He just expanded upon it."

"Humph."

"Steadman took the scavenger hunt game we played every Founder's Day and turned it into a week-long event. He even had an app created that leads tourists on a hunt all over the town in a geocaching style."

She gaped at Rick. "That's brilliant."

He nodded. "Every player has a chance to find a diamond, but only one is real. The rest are glass. A jeweler donates the real one. A black-tie event closes the week's festivities where an appraiser examines each stone and reveals who has the genuine gem. That's also the night of the art show where your cousin plans to feature Frankie's pictures."

"Wow, that's nothing like what we did on Founder's Day."

"I don't know; we did a lot of things on Founder's

Day."

A pretty flush spread up Jessie's neck. She certainly wasn't pale anymore. Did she remember the night they had teamed up and almost kissed? The only thing that stopped him was the fact Frankie would have clocked him for messing with his little sister.

Shortly after that night, the Berns family moved away, and he had always wondered what might have developed between them if they had been given a chance explore it. His gaze zeroed in on her lips, and his mouth dried up.

She cleared her throat. "Let's think less treasure hunter and more detective. Nancy Drew solved all her mysteries, right? Did she ever go up against a drug ring?"

Argh. She was worse than Max with a bone. "Don't know. I only read the Hardy Boys." He winked. "Tell me about travel writing, Nancy." He redirected her and ripped the garbage bags at the seams so they could open flat.

"I went to school and studied journalism. I wanted to be an investigative reporter but…" She shrugged apologetically. "…a girl's got to pay the bills. Besides, traveling the world, all expenses paid, is a pretty great gig. With Frankie…" She pulled her bottom lip into her mouth. "…unavailable, and Dad… MIA… it's not like I had anything holding me back." She said it with a smile, but the way it failed to light her eyes increased the ache in his heart. He remembered she had always planned to settle down and raise a family. And instead, she wandered the world like a nomad.

"Can you find some tape? Try the upper right drawer by the stove. That's a junk drawer."

She rummaged through the drawer by the stove while he tore open the remaining bags. She circled back to theorizing, and he had to admit that he loved how her mind worked. "Do you think the kids who let the dogs out are connected to this?" she said.

"What do you think?"

She dug deeper into the drawer. "Officer Thorn caught up with them. Those kids are students from the city. They're not from around here. Said they thought this place was a puppy mill with questionable practices. Seems they need to check their sources better. Someone fed them faulty information."

Rick made a note to check that. His gut told him someone had been watching them from the trees that night and those students would have had no reason to stick around.

"No comment?" She slammed the drawer closed with her hip and handed over a roll of duct tape.

"You're the one playing private investigator and theorizing. I'm just listening." He ripped off a strip of tape with his teeth and grabbed a bag, taping the bag to the window frame. "If you grab a hammer and nails, or a drill and some screws, I'll get this up and get out of your hair. There should be a box of tools in the spare room."

Her chin trembled. After what she'd been through, she had every right to be afraid at the thought of being alone. She went off in search of the tools.

God, I can't spend the night here, but I can't let her stay alone either.

She returned, lugging the toolbox, and dropped it at his feet. "This was easier than trying to find everything."

"You okay?"

She smiled, but it looked forced. "Yeah, it wasn't too heavy."

He wasn't asking about the toolbox, and the way she avoided his eyes told him that she knew it.

He snapped the proper bit onto the drill. "You shouldn't be alone tonight."

Something close to hope colored her expression.

"Is there anyone you can invite over for a few days?"

She turned to busy herself with some papers on the end table, but not quickly enough to hide her disappointment. "No one that I'd want to become target practice for a deranged hunter."

"Maybe you could stay with Steadman and Beth?"

"I'll be okay."

"You can always stay at my Aunt Norma's place." Aunt Norma had been a town mother to half the youth.

She'd open her place in a heartbeat.

"I'm not letting anyone push me out of Frankie's house... out of my house," she corrected. "I'm staying right here." Her words were unequivocal as she thrust her chin up in a stance of defiance.

He hoisted the first board up. She steadied one end while he drilled a screw through the other. "If you're staying here, I'll bunk out back in the kennel and leave Max with you. Once I give Max the command to guard, you'll be safe." If he didn't stay in the house, his presence wouldn't harm her reputation, and it would allow him to meet with Pete unnoticed.

She pressed her lips together. He didn't think she was going to say anything until a quiet "thank you" slipped out.

The rest of the boards went up quickly. He put the tools back into the case and snapped the lid shut. "You know, you theorize like a cop."

She flashed a cheeky grin, the first one tonight to make her eyes sparkle. "Or, like an investigative journalist."

She had some spunk. Nearly mauled by a dog, entangled in a drug scandal, threatened, attacked, and shot at—all on the heels of her brother's death. Many women would be rocking in the fetal position by now, but she hardly blinked. Jessie Berns wasn't just beautiful. She was a force to be reckoned with.

A force he couldn't become attached to. He better get

that through his head before his meeting with Pete. He had convinced Pete that Jessie was nobody special, and if Pete suspected anything different, he'd yank him from the case. He had a few hours to get his game face on and convince his boss that Jessie's presence wasn't an issue because no matter what Pete said, Rick wasn't going anywhere. She was Frankie's kid sister, and he would figure out what was going on even if it cost him his job. He owed that much to Frankie.

This Nancy Drew had met her Hardy Boy, whether she—or his handler—liked it or not. He was here to stay.

Chapter 6

Jessie flipped over in bed, and the old mattress frame groaned. She could have slept in the master bedroom. That room at least looked updated, and it probably even had a new mattress, but she couldn't bring herself to do it. In her mind, that space belonged to her dad, and walking back into this house made her feel like a teenager again. She naturally gravitated to her old bedroom. It was the room that felt safe, lumpy mattress and all.

She rolled onto her back and jammed the pillow under her head. Nothing helped. Probably because the problem wasn't the mattress or the room. The problem was the freak plotting his next attempt on her life. She stared at the ceiling and tried counting the swirls in the plaster pattern. Maybe it had to be sheep to work? She fumbled for her phone resting beside her Bible on the bedside table. 11:45 p.m.

Max lifted his head as if he sensed her restlessness.

She flung back her old quilt, swung her feet over the side of the bed, and slipped her toes into her slippers. She might as well make some herbal tea.

She snagged her Bible and puttered into the kitchen, flipping on lights as she went. Max obediently trailed her. He watched as she put the kettle on to boil, removed a mug from the cupboard, and tossed a tea bag into it. Max rubbed his head against her leg, and she dropped a hand to give his ears a scratch. Rick wasn't kidding when he promised the dog would guard her once given the command. She settled onto a kitchen chair and opened her Bible.

She didn't know where to start or what to pray, but she knew she needed the Lord.

When the pressure is on—pray. She'd jotted the note in the margin months ago on one of the few Sundays her traveling schedule had permitted her to attend Sunday services. In many ways, travel enhanced her faith. It allowed her to worship in many different settings and styles. At least that's what she told herself when feelings of guilt stirred regarding her inability to bond with a local church family. Every time she had the chance to open up to a person her words stuck in her throat. What if they weren't trustworthy? She always found an excuse to keep her distance.

She tried to calm her mind and find her usual comfort

in the presence of God, but the churning in her stomach wouldn't ease. She squeezed her eyes shut. *How much more, God? How much more will you ask from me?*

Everything changed when her dad was accused of stealing the pension money. *No sense staying where we aren't wanted,* Dad had said as their friends and neighbors turned them away. She had asked God to clear Dad's name. She had asked Him to let them stay in Chenaniah River, but God said no.

A tear dripped off her chin and splattered onto the pages of her opened Bible. Max lumbered over and put his head on her lap, his large, dark eyes conveying compassion.

Frankie's downward spiral started right after they moved. Dad had hit the road as a trucker with long day hauls. She tried to call him and explain what was going on, but there never seemed to be enough time to talk. She asked God to fix Frankie, to remove the pull of drugs and fast living. But again, God said no.

They stopped attending church. It was all Dad could do to put food on the table. No one knew them in the big city, or if they did, they didn't care about their well-being.

Eventually, she grew up. She left for school and made her way. Dad tried to reconnect at various points, and she knew that she needed to forgive him, but she couldn't get past her unanswered questions. Did Dad steal the money?

Why? How could he ruin their lives like that? They drifted apart, and she convinced herself that it was for the best.

You've already taken everything, God. My entire family is gone, and every time I ask you for something, you take me backward instead of forward.

She turned the pages in her Bible to the book of Joshua. Despite her questions, she couldn't deny her faith. Years of Sunday school and youth group had planted faith seeds so deep that even the worst drought hadn't shriveled them.

She fingered her necklace under the collar of her pajama top and flipped to chapter four. She recalled the day Grandma Annie explained the significance of her mother's pendant made of tiny stacked pebbles from the river. Passed down from daughter to daughter through their family, this 'pile of stones' was like the pile of stones the Israelites built in the Old Testament.

Jessie pulled the chain out from under the collar of her jammies and ran her fingers along the smooth edges. It was her reminder, Grandma had said, that women generations before her had been where she was, praying, waiting on God, and listening for His voice. It was her reminder that God always meets His people in their moment of need. Every time she saw it or touched it, she remembered that God answers prayer. But if Frankie's sober life was living proof of answered prayer, why was her proof now dead?

She dropped the necklace against her collarbone, and the weight of it burned. *Why, God?*

She tried to force her mind to focus on the words in front of her, but she kept replaying the last two days. Was the note on her car from someone warning her about danger or a ploy to leave her vulnerable to the attack? What did these people want from her? Did the sniper miss on purpose? Was he trying to scare her into leaving? Was she still in danger?

Max whimpered.

The kettle whistled.

She flipped the Bible closed. "Come on, Max. Do you need to go out?" She slid the kettle off the burner and glanced out the window toward the kennel.

Her neck hairs bristled. She squinted into the black night. Was that a person? A moonlit figure moved by the kennel window as a small flashlight beam bounced. Why weren't the motion lights working? She flicked on the porch light.

The shadow stilled and turned her way. It was a man! For one endless second, he pierced her soul with his stare. Jessie stabbed off the light and darkness cloaked her again.

She fumbled with the deadbolt on the back door and flung open the door. "Get him, Max," she repeated Rick's earlier command.

Max bolted after the fleeing man.

She pounded out Rick's cell number. *Thank you, Lord, that he had the sense to give it to me!*

No answer.

Max's barking faded. She turned off the electric fence to increase Max's chances of catching the guy. His barking now sounded like it was coming from the ravine and was getting closer to the river. She poked her feet into heavy boots and yanked on a jacket. She had to see if Rick was okay. She'd handled more than one overly aggressive suitor during her travels. A girl didn't safari alone in places like Africa without taking a few self-defense classes. She grabbed a baseball bat leaning against the wall near the back door just to be safe and activated her newly downloaded flashlight app on her phone to navigate her steps. She paused in the doorway. *Help me, Lord. Protect me.*

She crunched across the frosted ground. Yelping puppies sounded from inside the kennel. "Rick!" she hissed at the kennel door. She strained to hear him but couldn't make out anything over the ruckus the dogs created. She lifted the phone light to probe the shadows. "Rick? Are you here?" What if he was unconscious or hurt? She couldn't stand here and do nothing.

Glass crashed, and footsteps sounded behind the kennel. She pointed her light in that direction, but the beam wasn't powerful enough to reach the noise. She pressed her back against the kennel wall. She took a few deep breaths, gripping her bat tighter in one hand. *Help me, God.* She swung around and bounced a beam of light across the empty room. Did Rick leave on his own accord? Did the men send him running?

She retraced her steps back outside and studied the tracks in the snow. Her boot prints led from the house to here. Two different sets of prints and two different shoe sizes left the kennel from the front door. She circled to the back of the kennel and another set of prints led toward the river as if someone had escaped through the broken window. One set had to be Rick's, but there was no way to tell which set belonged to him.

With two uninvited guests on the property, she pressed 9 and 1 on her phone and hovered her thumb over the last 1, just in case. The men had to be gone by now; Max would have seen to that. But what if Rick was out here injured? She followed the prints to the ravine holding tight to her bat with one hand and swinging her flashlight back and forth with the other. She picked her way down to the river. Every snap of branches, whisper of wind, and rustling of evergreens boughs sent blood roaring through her ears.

Max's barking echoed through the woods. Just a little bit further, and she'd hit the clearing. The full moon should provide enough light to see once she got out from the bush. She tugged her coat tighter. She should have grabbed a scarf. Her flannel jammies and jacket offered little warmth.

She cleared the trees. Max raced across the footbridge spanning the river and was nearly on top of a man dressed all in black sprinting toward a snowmobile parked on the other side of the riverbank.

Come on, Max. She sprinted toward the river and skid to a stop at the edge. Would her phone's camera flash be enough for a picture? She had to try. She dropped the bat and raised the phone.

The man hopped aboard the snowmobile, and it roared to life. Max lunged but only snapped air as the machine pulled away.

She zoomed her camera lens into focus. A force from behind shoved her onto the frozen river. She landed hard on her hands and knees, and her phone shot across the ice.

Max barked.

The snowmobile zipped away.

A crack split the night, and the ice shifted beneath her.

Chapter 7

A splash of water doused a scream.

"Jessie!" Rick thrashed through the woods. Twigs scratched his face, and he swatted the branches away. He had heard the men poking around the kennels and managed to slip into the trees without being seen. He had wanted to watch them and learn what they were after, but Jessie interrupted when she let Max out.

He had watched her enter the kennel, calling his name from the tree line. When the second guy smashed through the kennel window and dashed into the woods, he couldn't let them both get away. He'd almost caught one of the men when Jessie broke through the trees. He had been too far away to stop a third man from rising up from behind her and shoving her onto the ice.

He hit the clearing. The river was dangerously quiet. Broken ice drifted down the center of the river, occasionally catching on the frozen edges of the bank. "Jessie!"

He yanked off his gloves and ripped a two-fingered whistle. Max came running.

"Where is she, Max?"

He dialed 9-1-1. "A woman has fallen through the Chenaniah River behind Frankie Berns's place."

"Medics are dispatched—"

"Help!"

He whipped around toward the sound. Where was she? He stuffed his phone into his pocket, leaving the connection active.

Rick sprinted toward the ice, skidding to a stop a few feet from the edge. Nothing but darkness and silence stretched before him. *Help me, God!*

A wet slosh and another cry ripped open the night.

Jessie burst through the water. She clawed the icy lip of the frozen river. "H-h-h-h-help!"

He gingerly stepped onto the ice, testing its ability to hold his weight. One step at a time, one inch at a time, he crept closer and closer to the edge. "Help is coming! Keep your head up!"

"I can't breathe—" Her raspy gasps punctured his heart. He had to reach her. She wouldn't last long enough for the help to arrive.

"You're hyperventilating." He crept closer. The ice

groaned. "Breathe deep and slow!" He stretched out flat over the icy surface, reaching out an arm just as her fingers gave way.

"No!" She plunged underneath the water.

She surfaced again, further back, bobbing downstream in the middle of the open water. Every edge she grasped shattered. Rick scampered back onto dry land.

"Swim to the side! Use your elbows to pull yourself up!" Rick rocketed down the embankment alongside her keeping pace with the current.

"I c-c-can't move my a-a-arms or l-l-legs."

She slipped under the surface again and took much longer to resurface this time. Rick bolted back to the trees. *Please, God, please!*

"Help!" Her desperate cry stabbed like a thousand knives.

He snapped a thick branch off a tree and darted back, thankful that full moon was bright enough to light the way. *God, show me where she is.*

Max yelped.

Jessie struggled about fifty meters down the river.

He barrelled down the riverside, getting ahead of her, and wrapped his arm around a tree trunk near the water's edge. He stretched out the branch. *Come on. Almost there.*

She swatted the tip and missed. She was too far away. *O God, I'm going to lose her, please no!*

"Max, jump!" he commanded.

Max leaped. The loose ice momentarily swallowed the dog. He burst up and paddled toward Jessie.

Her head bobbed, barely remaining above the surface. Water rolled over her face as the cold seemed to sap her strength. "Grab his collar!"

Her hand hardly broke the surface. "I can't."

"You have to, Jessie. Grab on!"

She wedged her hand between Max's collar and his neck.

"Good boy, Max! Come!"

Max tugged her in. As they neared the thin, frozen edge, Max clawed at the lip separating them from solid ground. It snapped off in chunks, and they plunged back into the deep, a tangle of paws, hands, and feet.

It was now or never. Rick crawled onto the ice, one tiny motion at a time, waiting for the crunch that sealed his doom. He spread out his weight, face down, and reached out his hands. Stories of heroes becoming victims bombarded his mind. *God, I can't do this alone.* He grabbed Max's collar and the back of Jessie's jacket and heaved them up onto their bellies, rolling them away from the thinner edge. He rolled until they hit the frozen dirt of dry land. For a half second, they lay there, piled in a tangled mess. They weren't out of danger yet. He dragged them off the ice and collapsed. *Thank you, Lord!*

His fingers trembled so violently that he struggled to peel off her sopping wet jacket and boots. Her eyes were closed. "Come, on, Jessie, stay with me."

He snapped up his phone. "I got her out. Where are the medics?" He unbuttoned his coat and tugged her close, pressing her back against his chest. He wrapped his arms and jacket around them both. A shock of cold shot through him as her soaking wet and freezing body leeched his heat. She was so cold. Too cold.

"They're on their way," the operator replied. "Do you have blankets or something warm to wrap her in?

"No."

Sirens wailed in the distance.

He punched speaker and set the phone down. Jessie's head rolled back onto his shoulder. Strands of frozen hair resisted his attempt to brush them off her pale, gray face. He rocked back and forth. *Lord, help me. Please, help me save her. I can't lose another woman, Lord. I can't.*

She'd lost her gloves. He covered her grayish fingers with his hands and rubbed furiously. Ice glistened in her eyelashes. Uncontrollable shivers rippled through her frame.

"Is she responding?" A voice shouted from the phone.

Jessie mumbled unintelligible words through bluish lips.

He almost wept at the sounds. "She's shivering and

mumbling."

"Shivering is a good sign. It means her body still has the energy to produce heat."

He pressed two fingers to her neck. "Her pulse is slow and weak. What's taking the medics so long?"

"Help is almost there," the maddeningly calm voice assured him. "Hold on."

Jessie's eyes sprang open and locked on him for a millisecond. Then, drifted shut.

"Jessie! Stay with me, Jessie. They're almost here," he whispered into her ear.

Her teeth chattered. "I s-s-aw s-s-someone."

He pressed his cheek against hers, willing his body heat to heal her. "Don't worry about that now."

The beautiful sounds of men thrashing in the woods broke the silence. "We're down here," Rick yelled.

Two paramedics and five firemen stormed the scene.

Rick nodded at the men he worked with every day and yielded Jessie to their care. He peeled himself away from her and stepped out of their way.

He scooped up his phone. "The medics are here. Thank you." He disconnected.

Someone threw a blanket over his shoulders.

After a crazy quick assessment, the medics tucked a blanket around Jessie and transferred her onto the scoop. "We gotta get her into the warm ambulance." They began the hike back up the treed slope to the waiting truck.

What if she didn't make it? What if he failed her too? Thank God for Max—*Max!*

Two firemen tended to Max, also suffering from the effects of the water. They wrapped him in a thick blanket, and Max soaked up the attention.

Rick stooped and peered directly into Max's eyes, scratching behind his ears with both hands. "Good boy, Max. Good dog."

"We'll see to him," the closest fireman promised. "We'll get him to the vet for you."

"Thanks." Rick could hardly push the thick word out his mouth. If it hadn't been for Max— He trotted after Jessie catching up at the truck. "What hospital are you taking her to?"

"Grand River Hospital," the closest medic responded.

"Is she going to make it?"

"She's conscious and talking. That's an excellent sign. Let's get her to the hospital. You can speak to us there."

Rick nodded. He pressed a hand on the man's back. "Her name's Jessie Berns. She's a friend of mine."

He nodded, understanding the unspoken.

Jessie's eyes fluttered open, and her gaze slammed into his. "You saved me," she slurred. She reached out a limp hand as the paramedics loaded her into the back of the ambulance. They brushed fingertips. How many times could he do this before her luck ran out?

Rick wanted to follow the ambulance, but he had to go back to the house to get his truck. He called Pete, who immediately left for the hospital. Ten eternal minutes later, Rick crashed through the hospital doors, and Pete jerked to attention from where he leaned against the wall.

"How is she?" Rick asked, as Pete fell into step beside him.

"They stabilized her in the ambulance. They're warming her, her pulse has come up, and her respiration has improved. They put her on oxygen, and her vitals are improving."

Rick inhaled his first full breath since the ambulance had zipped away. "Where is she now?"

"The doctors plan to do active rewarming. They'll run a heated IV through her to get some warm liquid into her body. The doc is going to come out when he can to update you."

Rick sagged. She was okay. She was going to be okay.

Pete studied him. He cupped his elbow with one hand and tapped his lips with the other. "Are you still going to try and tell me she's no one special?"

Rick swallowed. "You know who she is. She's Frankie's kid sister."

"Yeah, but who is she to you? You can't work this case if you're personally involved." His tone conveyed disapproval.

A few hours ago, Rick might have said that Jessie was just a buddy's sister. But now, he couldn't define who she was to him. His heart didn't usually jolt like this over a buddy or his sister.

Pete waited.

Rick didn't know what to say. It really didn't matter how much his heart heaved every time she walked into a room because his job prevented him from finding out if he could give her what she needed. He wanted to give Jessie more than the half-truths he could offer. She deserved more.

He collapsed into a padded chair, and the vinyl seat let out a whoosh of air. He pressed his knuckles into his neck muscles. If only it were as easy for him to decompress as the cushion. "She's a witness. She saw someone tonight."

Pete straightened. "Did you see him?"

"Not enough to describe him. There were three guys. I would have caught one if she hadn't been in the way."

"You gotta get that girl out of town before she gets herself killed," Pete said.

"That's my top priority. The funeral is only a few days away and then she'll be on her way."

While they waited for an update, they brainstormed. Who could have been poking around the kennel? Why? How did Jessie get involved and end up in the water? Rick filled Pete in on the $1500 monthly bank deposits and handed him the thumb drive from Daniel.

"This is from the parking lot. It captures the guy who left the note on her car and a second man who attacked her. We haven't been able to figure out who either one is. We are also trying to figure out who owns the car in the background, but we can't see the plates."

Pete shoved it into his pocket. "I'll see what I can do. When do you need it back?"

"I'll need to enter it into evidence soon."

They passed what felt like endless hours when the morning sun began its ascent over the horizon. A doctor finally came through the double doors. "Officer Chandler?"

He stood.

"I'm Doctor Smith. I've been taking care of Miss Berns. The nurse told me you were waiting for a report?"

"Yes, how is she?" The doctor's stoic expression offered no clue. Every nerve ending tingled.

"We'll keep her here throughout the day. Depending on her recovery, we may release her at the twenty-four-hour mark. But, considering that will bring us to nearly 1:00 a.m. tomorrow, we'll likely keep her until the following morning."

"Is she awake?"

"She was awake, but she's fallen asleep again. You

can see her if you like."

"I'm going to follow up on the things we discussed," Pete excused himself.

Rick nodded and followed the doctor into a nearby room.

The cold, white space chilled him like the river water. How did they expect to warm a patient suffering from hypothermia in such a sterile environment? The doctor tugged the curtain closed providing Rick some privacy.

Rick pulled up a chair as close to the bed as possible. Jessie's dark hair had thawed, and now lay brushed off her face in soft waves across the white pillowcase. He could almost imagine she was peacefully sleeping if he didn't dwell on the previous few hours.

He picked up her hand being careful not to disturb the IV dripping warm fluid into her body. He had come close to losing her tonight. It forced him to consider feelings he wasn't ready to consider.

Her eyelids fluttered.

"Jessie?"

She rolled her head toward his voice. "Hi."

"How do you feel?"

She didn't answer.

"I'm going to let the nurse know you are awake." Rick talked to the attendant at the desk, then he paced in the hallway waiting for the nurse to finish her assessment.

Waking again had to be a good sign.

"You can go in now." The nurse held the door open for him. "She's responding well. The doctor will be back to see her again now that she is fully alert, but you can visit until then. Don't be alarmed if she tires and needs to rest."

"Thank you."

"Why can't I go home?" Jessie asked the nurse before she could slip past Rick.

"The type of cold exposure you endured tonight can mess up your blood chemistry. You could form a blood clot, so we'll keep an eye on you for a bit yet."

Jessie's expression indicated it was not the answer she had hoped for, but she smiled anyway. "Thank you."

Rick reclaimed the chair by her bed but didn't pick up her hand again. "Sure is cold out there," he deadpanned. The corners of his lips twitched.

She flashed a crooked smile.

"Too soon?"

Her chuckle warmed him from the toes up. She always had a somewhat warped sense of humor. "I'm glad you're okay."

She plucked at the stiff bedsheet with her non-IV hand. "Thank you for saving me."

He scooped up her hand. It was so much warmer now that it shot pleasure through him. "Max saved you. He jumped in and swam you to shore."

"Max!" She jolted like she just remembered him. "How is he?"

"The firemen took him to the vet. He'll be fine. By the time you get home, he'll be there waiting."

"Thank you, Lord," she whispered. She sat back against her pillows.

He stroked her palm with the pad of his thumb. "What were you doing out there?"

She looked away as she tugged her hand back into her lap. "I saw someone. I tried to get his picture, but the phone fell into the river with me. At least I think it's in the river."

He scooted to the edge of his seat. If Jessie could describe the guy, maybe they could ID him. "Did he look like the man who left that note on your car?" She shook her head. "I couldn't see him well enough. It all happened so fast. It's a blur."

He leaned in. "You could have died tonight."

She fixed her eyes on her interlocked fingers on her lap. "It's not like I did it on purpose." She blinked rapidly.

Great. Now he'd made her cry. "Hey, it's going to be okay. We'll figure out what's going on."

"Where is she?" An authoritative voice blasted through the hallway.

Rick rose from the chair, but Jessie latched onto his forearm. "It's okay. It sounds like Steadman."

Steadman and his wife, Beth, burst into the room.

"Are you okay?" Beth immediately perched on the side of the bed and picked up Jessie's hand, forcefully nudging Rick out.

"I'm fine."

Steadman settled his fierce gaze onto Rick. "Why didn't anyone call me?"

Rick straightened. "I didn't know you expected notification. It's my understanding you haven't been close the last ten years."

"That's uncalled for—"

"I'm sorry, Steadman," Jessie interrupted. "I just woke up. You're here now." She looked at Beth. "That's what matters."

Steadman shifted his gaze to Jessie, and his eyes softened. "And we're not going anywhere. Beth and I will help you recover, so you won't miss your flight to Africa to cover that safari for the magazine."

She pulled her hand from Beth's grasp and threaded her fingers in her lap. "I might cancel the trip. An investigative journalist doesn't walk away from a possible story. There's a story here."

"You're not an investigative journalist," Rick interjected. "You're a travel writer who literally fell in over her head." As much as he'd like to keep her around, he'd rather she be touring the African jungle than poking her nose into a case that could get her murdered.

Jessie turned her head away. "If only I didn't drop my phone, maybe we'd have a picture and could end this."

"That's the least of your worries," Beth said as she fussed with the bedsheets covering Jessie.

Jessie huffed. "I had everything on that phone. All my work contacts. Everything."

"I'll go to the house as soon as it's light out and see if I can find it," Beth offered. "Maybe it didn't go into the river. Maybe it's on the river bank or something."

"Thank you." Jessie smiled tiredly.

"We should let you rest." Rick stood, hoping Steadman and Beth would follow suit.

"He's right, sweetheart. You need your rest. We don't want to lose you, too." Beth blinked fast like she was blinking back tears.

"Someone's been targeting me ever since I returned to town. I don't need to rest. I need to know why." Jessie's eyes flashed indicating that she was beginning to feel better. Some of her spunk had returned.

"We just don't want you to get hurt," Steadman said gently.

She looked out the window. "I'm already hurt."

Chapter 8

A sad melody of appropriate funeral hymns played through the church sound system as whispered conversations filled the sanctuary. Rick stood at the back wishing he could sit with Jessie in the front pew reserved for family. Steadman and Beth sat on her right, but somehow, she still looked alone. His insides battled between wanting to offer her comfort and needing to scrutinize people as they arrived. He nodded at Sam Bommel and his brother, Derek, as they found seats behind Gavin and his wife, Kenzie.

Jessie fiddled with her necklace of pebbles.

If Aunt Norma were here, she'd ignore the reserved-for-immediate-family sign and sit with them. Maybe Aunt Norma would arrive before the service started.

Pastor Carl stepped to the podium. "Let's pray."

So much for Aunt Norma. Rick closed the back double-doors to the sanctuary.

After Pastor Carl had finished praying, Rick scooted into the empty spot on Jessie's left. She didn't say anything, and she didn't have too. The gratefulness in her eyes said enough. He nodded in acknowledgment.

The sanctuary easily sat 300 people, but today, less than a hundred congregated to remember Frankie's life. A smattering of Frankie's old friends, who still lived under the influence and control of drugs and alcohol, shifted noisily on the hard, wooden-bench seats. Their discomfort likely had more to do with entering the house of God than the bench itself.

Jessie leaned over as if to say something when her eyes widened. A familiar minty scent settled into the pew beside him.

"How are you, dear?" Aunt Norma's silvery whisper carried the faintest hint of peppermint candy.

"Thank you for coming." Jessie's eyes glistened.

"Of course, I came." Aunt Norma nodded at Steadman. "Mayor Munroe. Beth."

Rick's aunt wiggled around as if she couldn't get comfortable until she nudged Rick thigh to thigh with Jessie. Aunt Norma had a matchmaking streak. He wouldn't put it past the usually punctual woman to have lingered in the restroom until he plunked himself down beside Jessie. His leg tingled where it brushed against the delicate folds of Jessie's skirt.

"Thank you for sitting with me," Jessie murmured in his ear. "I didn't know it would be so..." her words broke off.

He enclosed her tiny palm in his hand and ignored his earlobe that burned from her whisper. He was just being a good friend. "Anytime." He gently squeezed her fingers. Her eyes softened, and she turned her attention back to the front but didn't withdraw her hand.

A satisfied smile crept across Aunt Norma's face.

A handful of Frankie's new friends, representative of his presence in recovery meetings and Bible studies, nodded along with Carl's declarations of God's goodness in the midst of confusion and suffering. Glaringly absent were Frankie's parents. His mother had died when Jessie was born, but what kind of father didn't come to his kid's funeral? He tightened his hold on Jessie's hand, and she leaned into him ever so slightly.

Her eyes sparkled against her jewel-toned sweater and black skirt. Her pale skin glowed with a glamorous old movie star style that even her grief couldn't conceal. He looked down at their entwined fingers.

His vow to remain "just friends" wavered. He stiffened. She was his buddy's sister. Frankie would want Rick to keep her safe and be her friend not mess with her heart. Besides, he couldn't afford to get emotionally involved with a person of interest in his investigation. It would cloud his objectivity. He gave her fingers a final squeeze and pulled his hand free.

She kept her attention on the pastor. If she was disappointed at his withdrawal, she didn't show it.

Aunt Norma, however, huffed.

"Many of you have special memories of Frankie," said Pastor Carl. "The one I cherish is how this man changed when he turned from his sins. He accepted responsibility for his actions and worked hard to right his wrongs. His final year of life was a living testimony of God's power to transform a willing heart. Frankie refused to define himself by his mistakes; he instead defined himself by his Savior. If Frankie were here today, he would ask what or who defines you?"

Rick shifted. Does a man after God secretly investigate his fellow officers? He essentially lived a double life, one that Jessie didn't even know about. He shoved the uncomfortable thoughts down and scanned the crowd. Finding one of the men who accosted Jessie in the parking lot would be their best lead. There was a slim chance he'd show his face here today.

The double doors that separated the foyer from the sanctuary bumped open, and a puff of coolness swirled around Rick's feet. Someone had slipped in late. A hood covered most of the man's profile, and a puffy blue winter jacket hid his frame. He slouched into the sanctuary and settled into a back row well behind the others. He kept his head down, but his eyes darted all around the room before resting on Jessie a bit too long.

Rick leaned to whisper into Jessie's ear, and a whiff of lilac caught him by surprise. His lip tingled where it grazed her lobe. "I have to see to something."

Her neck reddened, and for the briefest second hurt flashed across her face, but she replaced it with acceptance.

"I'll be right back," he promised. Only a rat would leave her in the middle of the service, but she'd understand when he had the opportunity to explain.

He ignored Aunt Norma's disapproving glare and Steadman's judgmental one as he excused himself. He walked toward the back for a better view of the stranger's face. If the guy turned out to be an old friend who was here to pay his respects to Frankie, Rick wouldn't disturb him. But something about the shifty way the stranger sized up the room sent Rick's radar humming.

The man's roving gaze locked with Rick's for a millisecond. He zipped it away.

Gotcha! Rick pulled back his jacket flap and flashed the badge on his hip. "Can you come with me, please?"

The mystery man slid obediently out of his seat and exited the sanctuary. As soon as the interior doors shut behind him, he broke into a sprint and bolted across the foyer. He exploded through the exterior doors onto the street.

Rick raced after him. He leaped down the outer church steps, absorbing the impact with his knees. He scanned throngs of people littering the sidewalks. Chenaniah River was days into the Winter Diamond Festival, and the town had swelled with treasure hunters searching for the lost diamond.

There. A flash of blue. The hunched-over, hooded man threaded his way upstream through the pedestrians swarming the downtown core. The runner never looked back. He bobbed and weaved through the crowd with purpose and speed like he had planned his escape.

Innocent men don't plan their escape.

Rick slammed into two teens exiting Forever Christmas. The impact scattered their shopping bags. "Sorry!"

He spun around them, losing his visual. Where'd he go? Rick paced the sidewalk, peering into storefronts and alleys. He stopped in front a pretzel vendor near the outdoor ice rink. Business owners erected colored tents outfitted with portable heaters in preparation for the day's festivities. The center hummed with life.

Another flash of blue. This time from the other side of the ice rink. He slip-slided his way across just in time to see the man spin a wide-eyed teenager aside and duck past her into a back alley.

He caught the arm of the stunned woman. "You okay?"

She nodded.

"Call the police," he called over his shoulder. "Tell them an officer is in pursuit of a suspect." He drew his weapon and flattened himself against the storefront nearest the alley and peeked around the edge. No one. Rick stepped out. He eyeballed the deserted space moving from garbage bins to doorways to any nook capable of concealing a man. He cleared them one by one reaching the end of the alley empty-handed.

Come on, God, a little help here.

Rick holstered his gun and retraced his steps back to the church. He had no official charge against the man, yet his build was similar to the man who slipped the note under Jessie's wiper blade but that broke no laws. Still, innocent people don't run. His instincts told him this guy knew something about Frankie.

The mourners clustered around a graveside in the cemetery adjacent to the church. He'd missed the entire service. Rick immediately sought out Jessie's familiar red coat and exhaled relief. Aunt Norma had a protective arm around her shoulder, and Jessie stood sandwiched between her and Beth. His tension drained until a flash of blue stirred the crowd a few people behind them. The guy had circled back? Was he going to hurt Jessie?

"Jessie!" Rick sprinted.

She turned at his call.

His lungs seared from the chase. He had failed Frankie. He would not fail Frankie's sister. The runner bolted again.

Rick sprung over headstones and dodged keepsakes marking graves. The distance between them closed just as they were about to exit the cemetery gates. Rick had him. "Stop! Police!"

The man slowed just outside the entrance. He raised his hands, his chest heaving.

Rick approached, one hand hovering over his gun and the other extended in front of him. The man's gaze flicked to the right.

An elderly couple, carrying flowers, rounded the corner.

"Look out!" Rick's warning came too late.

The man bolted between them, knocking the woman on the slippery sidewalk, so her husband clutched her arm to keep her upright.

Rick steadied the two as his target escaped. "Are you okay?"

"Yes, thank—"

Rick didn't wait. Years of training kicked in, and Rick gained on the man who was now losing speed. A burst of adrenaline shot through him. He dove, taking the man down. He landed on his shoulder and rolled on top of the perpetrator. No way would he let this guy hurt Jessie. No way. "You're under arrest."

"She can't see me. She can't know that I'm here." The man struggled against Rick, nearly throwing him off balance.

Rick pressed his knee into the man's back and zip-tied his wrists together. "Who can't see you?" He had a sick feeling he already knew the 'she' to whom he referred, but he needed to hear him say the words.

"Jessie."

Rick hauled the wannabe stalker to his feet and got right in his face. "What's your interest in her?"

He held Rick's gaze. It wasn't the defiant glare of the guilty. It held steady and sincere. "I'm her father." Tension radiated off the man who bore little resemblance to Jessie's dad, Jack Berns.

Rick's fist, bound up in the man's coat, tightened. "Jack left years ago."

"I know. Frankie and I reconnected when he got sober. I've been helping him with the kennel."

Jack reappeared, and Frankie was suddenly dead? Rick twisted his fist deeper into the down-filled jacket. He wasn't buying it. "You can tell me everything at the station."

Jack pulled away.

Rick yanked him back. Hard.

"You can't take me there!" Jack's clenched mouth set off a twitch in his cheek. Rick could have counted Jack's heartbeats through that twitch if he wanted to.

"Give me one good reason why not."

"If you bring me in, they'll kill me to keep me quiet." Jack's entire body vibrated in Rick's hands.

"Who will kill you?"

Jack looked him right in the eye. "The same people who killed Frankie. I think they're after Jessie, too."

"You got a name?" Rick growled.

"The Chenaniah police."

Jessie said goodbye to Aunt Norma, who only left after Jessie promised to stop by for a visit sometime soon. She sank onto one of the gray stacking chairs in the fellowship hall tucked into the basement of the church. She was glad today was almost over. Across the room, Steadman and Beth chatted with a few lingering visitors. She needed this sweet moment of reprieve.

Just outside the basement window, the booted feet of people enjoying the Winter Diamond Festival scurried down the sidewalk. Bitterness rose like bile up her throat. How dare they parade around town, laughing and smiling, trying to win that silly diamond? Time did march on, not stopping for anything or anyone.

"Jessie?" Beth perched in front of her wearing an expectant expression.

She blinked. "I'm sorry, I didn't hear you."

Beth's motherly smile plucked Jessie's heart. "I asked if you planned to stay in town long."

"I don't know." Her gaze drifted back to the window. She had just sold her editor a story about the town's festival. Should she forget about it and just leave? It seemed to be what everyone wanted. What was here for her now anyway?

"Why don't you come and stay at our place until you decide? It'll be easier than staying at your old house."

"That's kind, but I need to sort Frankie's things and take care of the dogs."

Beth wrinkled her nose. "Oh right. The dogs. You shouldn't have to do that alone."

"She won't have to." Steadman rested a hand on his wife's shoulder. "Tell us how we can help you."

Jessie considered it. There was a massive amount of work involved with selling the business, not to mention listing the house. Her gaze kept wandering to the window. She half-hoped she'd see Rick hauling back the man he had chased from the graveside. She didn't know why she kept looking for him. It wasn't like she'd recognize him by his boots anyway.

A small gray hatchback rolled in front of the window and idled across the street.

Jessie repositioned herself for a better view just as it pulled away. Did it have a bumper sticker? Was it the same car she'd seen before? She couldn't tell.

"You look tired dear. Have you had anything to eat?"

She shook her head. "I'm fine."

Beth stood and motioned to her husband that it was time to go. "Why don't you pack up and get some rest?" She and Steadman had never had children. Beth seemed to thrive in this new motherly role.

"I think I will. Thanks for coming. We'll do that dinner real soon."

A noisy growl ripped through her stomach as she waved goodbye. She pressed a hand to her gut. She massaged her abdomen in rhythmic circles while straining for another glimpse of the car. Her head throbbed.

Someone had opened a window. The scent of pine needles swirled through the room and stirred the air. Was it from the nearby trees? Rick wore pine-scented aftershave.

A gentle hand squeezed her shoulder. "When was the last time you ate something?"

Rick! Her stomach fluttered. *He came back.*

He pulled up a chair and sat across from her.

"I'm not sure." She looked for her purse. She kept a stash of protein bars in there, and she needed one just as much as she needed to pull the plug on the electricity sparking between them. "Have you seen my purse?"

"No."

"Who was that guy you chased? Did he have something to do with Frankie?"

"Let me help you look." It didn't escape her attention that he avoided her question. She considered mentioning the car, but if he didn't want to talk about the case, she'd wait until he did. She didn't have the energy to force it.

"I left it right here during the interment." She pointed at the long table sitting under the window. At least, she thought she had left it there. She moved through the scattered chairs. Had she moved it and forgotten?

The two of them searched the hall, the sanctuary, and even retraced their steps to the graveside. No luck. How could she be so stupid? A lot of Frankie's old friends, some still using, had come today. A junkie picked an unattended purse like a farmer picked ripened fruit. Even if there was little cash, addicts could use credit cards to buy merchandise they could later pawn. A crushing weight squeezed the air from her lungs. On top of everything else, she would need to cancel all her cards.

"I had everything in my purse," she moaned.

"Sit down, let me get you some water." Rick returned

with a glass and a plate of sandwiches. He placed them on the table in front of her and gestured that they were for her. "Your purse has to be here. We'll find it."

"Thank you." She drank deep. Her stomach growled again, and heat flushed her cheeks at the embarrassing noise. "I wasn't able to tolerate the idea of food despite how much Aunt Norma and Beth tried to get me to eat."

She eyed the plate of sandwiches. One looked like tuna, the other like egg salad. She had told the caterer about her coconut allergy when she arranged the menu. Everything was supposed to be nut free, but she was always careful about her diet.

"If I could just find my purse, I keep protein bars in there." Her gut clenched in protest. She needed food. She lifted the bread and sniffed the filling. "Nut allergy," she reminded Rick when he raised his eyebrows.

"A boy who attends here has a severe allergy. We are a nut free facility."

"We?"

"This is my church."

Interesting. So, was he a man of faith or a bench warmer?

She had heard about their nut policy when she spoke with the church about bringing in a caterer. Her stomach growled again. She could ask Rick to drive her home, but that would take another fifteen minutes. She eyed the plate of food again. It should be safe. She popped a quarter of the crustless sandwich into her mouth. Food would help ease the pounding in her head. She popped in another and took a swig of water.

"Should we fill out a report about the purse?" Rick asked.

"I don't—" Her tongue started to tingle, and a lump rose in her throat. She pushed the plate away from her. It slid over the table edge and crashed to the floor. She reared upright, toppling the chair behind her. Her palms itched, and her scalp began to prickle. Stars flashed. A hot and sweaty wave rolled over her.

Rick jumped up only a few beats behind her. "What's wrong? Are you choking?" His words hardly registered over the thundering in her ears.

She clawed her throat, gasping against the rising pressure. She looked wildly around the room. Her EpiPen was in her purse! She had to find it.

"Epi. Pen. Purse." She couldn't get enough oxygen.

Her vision narrowed into a blackened pinpoint. She swayed, and then doubled over and retched.

"What's going on?" Pastor Carl thundered into the deserted room.

"She's anaphylactic! We need an EpiPen!"

Jessie's knees gave out, and she collapsed. The cool floor pressed against her.

"Call 9-1-1." Rick's voice echoed through her head.

The concrete floor did little to relieve the raging fire coursing through her veins. Something pressed against her face. It irritated her burning skin.

"Jessie, Jessie, stay with me!"

Rick was here. Rick would help her.

"Where are you going?" Rick yelled at someone, but she couldn't remember who else had been in the room. She didn't even care. An unrelenting weight pressed the air from her lungs. Her eyelids fell into a long and cumbersome blink. *Am I going to die?*

She peeled her eyes open just as Carl thrust something into Rick's hand.

A sudden pressure slammed into her thigh. Then, another slam. Within a minute the caustic acid burning through her insides flooded with a refreshing coolness.

She opened her eyes. The fuzz slowly cleared. The boulder in her throat dissipated, and she gulped in air. *Thank you, Lord.*

"Are you okay? Can you talk?" Rick's face swam in front of her.

"Is she going to be okay?" Carl asked.

Rick and Carl hovered. A siren sounded in the distance. She nodded.

"I'll get the paramedics." Carl rushed upstairs.

Jessie accepted Rick's help getting up and relocating

to a chair. She rubbed her thigh near the puncture mark. There'd be a killer bruise there tomorrow. "Did you inject me twice?"

Rick's eyes relaxed at her question, but his body remained tight and alert. "Carl brought two junior pens. One of the kitchen volunteers has a son with severe allergies. She had the pens in her purse. They are a half dose each, so I gave you a double hit."

"Lucky me. Two bruises." Her joke fell flat.

Carl ushered the paramedics into the basement.

The medics fussed over her, checking her blood pressure and levels. This wasn't her first rodeo with an EpiPen, but they still insisted on bringing her to the hospital.

Carl and Rick spoke in hushed voices a few steps away. She caught the word premeditated. Rick gestured to the sandwich he had bagged. When they noticed her approach, the conversation ceased.

She rolled her eyes. "Look, I'm not a kid. I can handle whatever it is you're talking about." Rick hesitated just long enough to make her want to stamp her foot, but that would counter her claim to be an adult.

"Your purse with the EpiPen, was stolen right before you had an allergy attack. This wasn't an accident."

Jessie's knees weakened.

Rick cupped her elbows and eased her into a chair. A

warm feeling of safety coursed through her.

"Could that man be behind this? The man you chased out of here?" She tried to remember his face but couldn't. Was it the injections or Rick's warm grasp that made her mind fuzzy?

"That's what I plan to find out."

"You ready to go?" The medic tapped his foot by the doors leading upstairs.

Jessie stood. "I saw a dark gray car through the window earlier, but I couldn't tell if it was the same one I saw at the police station."

Rick's eyes darkened. "It isn't safe for you here."

She bristled. She'd already given her African travel assignment to another writer and pitched a new story to her editor. Chenaniah River's reinvention into a tourist town after the collapse of industry excited her editor. She loved the Winter Diamond Festival, the art show, and how people traveled from all over to take part in a treasure hunt that directed ninety-nine percent of the people to hidden fake diamonds and one lucky winner to a real one. Jessie couldn't leave now even if she wanted to. It would cost her job.

"Ms. Berns?" The medic rested his hands on his hips.

"I'm coming." At least she'd be safe at the hospital.

Chapter 9

"Where is he?" Rick slammed the front door of the safe house so hard the single pane glass in the windows rattled. He tossed his drenched jacket across the back of the old plaid couch and strode to the kitchen, leaving a wet boot-printed trail. Pete looked up from the papers strewn on the scuffed up wooden table, and Jack Berns tensed.

Pete's chair scratched the faded linoleum floor as he pushed himself up.

"What's your end game, Jack?" Rick's entrance infused the room with instant tension. He flexed and extended his fingers at his sides. They itched to strike someone, anyone, to relieve the pressure building inside of him. His heartbeat thundered in his ears. Jessie's dad was tied up in this mess somehow, and Rick had to find out how before someone killed her.

Jack half rose from his chair, fists clenched like he was

ready for whatever Rick gave, but Pete motioned for him to sit back down. Jack raked his eyes up and down Rick before sitting. "I don't know what you're talking about. I don't have an end game."

"You better not be messing with me." Rick hovered over Jack and jabbed his finger in his chest.

"This isn't the way," Pete cut in.

Pete was right. Rick let out a slow breath between clenched teeth. Intimidating Jack wouldn't solve anything, and it wouldn't plug the gushing fear of seeing Jessie asphyxiating and not being able to stop it. Logic dictated that Jack wasn't involved since he was here with Pete, but Jack sure made an easy target for his wrath.

Rick rummaged in his pocket and tossed a plastic wrapped sandwich on the table.

"What's that?" Jack lifted his chin toward the sandwich.

"I suspect it is coconut laced tuna intended to kill Jessie."

"What?" Jack shot up so fast that the chair behind him toppled. "Is she okay? Where is she?"

Pete righted the chair and forced Jack back onto his seat. He motioned for Rick to take the chair across from him. He stood over them like a hockey referee ready to pull apart two fighting players. He picked up the bag and studied the contents. "Walk us through it."

Rick recapped the events as succinctly as possible.

"And the police let you take this?" Pete turned it over in his hand.

"No, they took the other half of the sandwich, the half she bit into. They'll run some tests, but I grabbed the rest of it, so we can run our own tests."

"This is all my fault." Jack cradled his head in his hands.

Rick flicked his gaze to Jack. "Explain that."

Jack looked up. For the first time, Rick really saw him. Dark rings circled his eyes, deep wrinkles folded into creases, and leathery skin sagged from years of outdoor work. This wasn't a criminal mastermind. This was a beaten man, a desperate man. Rick narrowed his eyes. Desperate men were the hardest to read.

"The allergies and asthma run through my side of the family. Both kids inherited them through me." Jack dragged a hand down over his face. "Where is Jessie now? Can I see her?"

Rick softened, but only a little. "She's at the hospital getting checked out."

"It was smart, getting your own sample." Jack nodded toward the sandwich. "You can't trust the local lab. Not if you want real answers. The cops are up to their eyeballs in this. I know it."

"I'm beginning to think you're right." Rick nodded.

"What else have you uncovered?" Pete furrowed his eyebrows. A gut feeling wouldn't be enough for Pete. He needed facts.

"Nothing you don't already know," Rick had to admit, "but when I add up everything that has happened, it doesn't look good for the police."

Pete raised a brow.

"The night Jessie rolls into town half the force shows up at her place. The chief is *in the neighborhood.*" Rick put air quotes around the words. "Then he acts like he has something to hide. The same car spotted in the police parking lot when Jack stuck the note on Jessie's car *happens* to be in the area the night someone takes a shot at her through her kitchen window. Again, the entire police force seems to respond. Gavin even brought wood to repair the broken window. My gut tells me something is not right. No one gets this much attention unless something else is going on." He ticked the coincidences off on his fingers.

"Promise me you'll keep my girl safe." Jack leaned across the table and looked earnestly into Rick's eyes.

"Your girl? She hasn't been your girl in years, Jack. You can't play the father card now after all this time and expect it to hold any weight."

Jack winced.

Jack might be a lousy father but years in the field had taught Rick to trust his gut. His gut said there was something to Jack's fears about the police. That was the only reason he called in Pete when he caught Jack at the funeral. Pete took him into RCMP custody instead of hauling him into the police station.

Pete tapped a recorder app on his phone and placed it on the table between them as Rick picked up the notepad from the table and flipped it open. "Tell us what you know about Frankie's death." Jack folded his hands in front of him on the table. "Frankie called me the day he died. Said some old man from the senior home had pressed pills into his hands, muttering something about how he was sorry it was late. It wasn't the first time that happened."

Rick and Pete looked at each other. So, Jack knew about the drugs. Rick had been on his way to collect the evidence the day Frankie had died, but instead of bagging evidence, he had to bag the body of his childhood friend. The drugs were never seen again until that bottle turned up in Jessie's purse.

"Don't you get it?" Jack's fingers, threaded together, tightened until the skin turned white. "The police were the only other people he told."

"What about that note you left Jessie?" Rick interjected.

Jack released his fingers and dragged one hand through his greasy hair. "I didn't mean to scare her with the note, but Jessie needed to know the police couldn't be trusted. When I saw her with him…" He nodded to Rick. "…I had to warn her. Whatever Frankie got into, it was bad. I don't want it finding her."

"It's already found her," said Rick.

Jack's eyes darkened.

"Why didn't you come forward?" Pete asked.

"Forward to who? The police? They killed Frankie."

"You could have come to me. Frankie and I go way back. You know that."

Jack finally looked at Rick, his face lined with weariness and grief. "You? You're the officer famous for shirking the rules and letting his informants down. And at the end of the day, you wear the same uniform as the guys who killed my son. You're either one of two things: incompetent or involved."

Rick fisted his hands under the table but forced his expression to remain neutral. Jack wasn't the first guy to try and get under his skin during an interrogation.

"So, which is it?" Jack pressed.

Would he ever recover from Anderson's smear campaign? "How about you judge my integrity and ability by the fact I've saved Jessie's life more than once. By the fact I called in Pete, who brought you here, not to the station."

A hint of a smile turned up Jack's lips as if he liked the fire he lit inside of Rick. Jack shifted his gaze to Pete. "I gave Frankie the money he needed to start his business, but we kept it from Jessie."

Rick jotted down the information. "Why?"

"Because she wouldn't acknowledge or return any of my attempts to reconnect with her. I knew she'd think that I had bought Frankie's forgiveness, and I didn't want that. I wanted her to see that I earned it."

"How much were you giving him?" Pete asked.

"I sent him $1500 every month. Cash. Untraceable."

That cleared up the large lump sum deposits into Frankie's account.

"It took a long time for Frankie to trust me again. I was on my way up here to see the place when he phoned about the drugs. He was all panicked like no one would believe they weren't his."

"What did you tell him?" Pete asked.

"I told him to call the cops. Be honest and up-front like the honorable man he was trying to become."

The word honorable hit Rick like a fist to the gut. No one in the general public viewed him as honorable anymore. Not after Anderson had finished with him.

"Did Frankie make that call then?" Rick didn't remember seeing a notation anywhere on Frankie's file about a call to the police about the drugs.

"Definitely. We hung up, and then I called back fifteen minutes later to ask what he did. He said he called and that someone was coming over, and in the meantime, he had stashed the drugs somewhere safe."

Pete lifted a curious brow.

Rick nodded, affirming silently that he was the 'someone' coming over. Frankie had never called the actual police.

Jack continued, "Then the doorbell rang."

"Did he say who it was?" Rick looked up from his notes.

"No, but he called him 'officer,' then there was some scuffle, and the phone dropped."

"But I never spoke with—"

Pete's hand shot up and cut Rick off. "Was the call still engaged?"

"Yeah," Jack's voice caught. "I heard the whole thing." Grief darkened his eyes as he relived the last moments of Frankie's life.

"What exactly did you hear?" Rick's insides softened just a bit. Whether he liked the man or not, Jack was still a father grieving his son.

"It was muffled." Jack swiped across his eyes with his sleeve. "Like they had walked away from the phone or something. Someone asked Frankie what he knew and where it was."

"Knew about what? What were they looking for?" Pete pressed.

"I don't know. The drugs? The guy repeated his questions. There was another scrimmage of some sort, then I heard Frankie wheezing."

"Wheezing?" Rick flashbacked to Jessie struggling to breathe. Whoever was behind this knew the Berns family well enough to play their weaknesses against them.

"Yeah, wheezing like he needed his inhaler."

"You're sure?" Pete asked.

Jack lifted his head to meet Pete's gaze. "You don't raise a son with asthma and not memorize the sound of him fighting for breath. It's not something you ever forget."

"Then what happened?"

"The man shouted, 'Tell me where it is, and you can have it.'"

"Have what?"

Jack sniffed. "I'd guess his inhaler."

"Then what?"

"I heard banging, like Frankie was opening and closing drawers. The guy laughed and said that he had them all. Then, a thump," Jack's voice caught, "like a body hitting the floor."

"I knew the fact that there were no inhalers in the house was significant. But when I brought it up, I was dismissed."

"By who?" Jack narrowed his eyes.

"Gavin had convinced the chief it wasn't relevant due

to Frankie's history of negligence."

"It's time to take a closer look at Gavin," Pete said.

Jack's quiet sobs shook his body. This wasn't a man involved in his son's death, not unless he was a Grammy award-winning actor. So, it was unlikely that he was a threat to Jessie. "Did you hear anything else?"

"Whoever was there found the phone. He cursed as he picked it up. He asked if anyone was there."

"What did you do?" Pete asked.

"I disconnected."

"Why did you hide?" asked Pete.

Jack had lost all cockiness and looked every inch a beaten man who'd choose differently if he could go back and do life over. "If a member of the Chenaniah Police Force watched my son die, what would stop him from tracing my number and coming after me? I couldn't go home. They'd kill me too. But I couldn't leave either, not once Jessie arrived."

Pete stopped the recording. "Stay here." He motioned for Rick to follow him into the other room. "What do you think?"

Rick braced both hands against the back of the couch and stretched out his tense arm muscles. "I don't believe he's a threat to Jessie."

"Me either." Pete nodded. "But, if his theory is right, he's a target for whoever is behind this."

"What do we do?"

"For now, keep Jack our little secret."

Rick's eyes widened. "Even from Jessie?"

"Yes. We need to keep this quiet. The fewer people who know, the better, especially if this goes as deep as I suspect."

How was he supposed to keep something like this from Jessie?

"That also means that thumb drive can't get logged into evidence." Pete held up the thumb drive Rick had turned over the night they spent in the hospital waiting room. "We can't take the chance someone else will identify Jack leaving the note."

"How do I explain that to the chief?"

"Hopefully, no one will look for it, and it won't be an issue." Pete pressed it into Rick's hand. "Sit on it for as long as possible." Rick nodded.

"We'll keep Jack here, in the safe house," Pete said.

"What about Jessie? What do I tell her?"

"You need to get that girl out of here. Tell her whatever it takes to accomplish it."

Rick snorted, "I've been trying. Short of tying her up and tossing her in my trunk and driving out of town, there's not much I can do. Not without telling her the truth."

"Don't tell her that. Not yet."

That was easy for Pete to say. He didn't have a

friendship that went back years with her. Jessie was going to freak out when she learned that her dad was back and that Rick knew about it but didn't tell her. But if their friendship had to take a hit to keep her safe, so be it. Her life mattered more.

The face of every local officer passed through Rick's mind. If Jack was right, the Chenaniah River Police Force employed a murderer who worked alongside Rick every day. Could Rick catch him before he killed again?

Chapter 10

The steady rain calmed Jessie's nerves. The repetitive percussion of the drops slapping the windshield soothed her anxiety.

"At least the freezing rain held off long enough for the cemetery service." Rick upped the speed of the wiper blades, and the rhythmic thud-thud of the rubber sliding across the windshield joined the pinging sound of rain splatter.

The funeral felt like days ago, but it had only been that morning. Jessie looked out the window, too tired for small talk. The hospital had finished with her relatively quickly, but she'd had to wait an additional thirty minutes for Rick to pick her up. While she waited, she recapped her time back in Chenaniah River. It was hard to believe she'd been in town for only four days. Since her Sunday arrival, she'd been questioned by the police, shot at, submerged under ice, admitted to the hospital and then discharged twice. She'd also buried her brother—all without the help of her parents.

"You okay?" Rick reached across the interior of the car and rested his hand on hers. His eyes softened as he studied her.

"Just thinking about Mom and Dad."

He pulled his hand away, and she immediately missed the warmth of his touch.

"Do you think Dad even knows Frankie is dead?" The ache for a mom she never knew always throbbed, but her longing for family had spiked as she sat in that pew this morning grieving Frankie without Dad. Having Steadman and Beth helped, and when Rick and Aunt Norma joined her, the weight of loneliness lifted a bit more but not entirely. She didn't think the oppressive heaviness would ever fully lift.

"I think he'd want to be here for you if he could."

She pressed her fingers to her smiling lips. It was a sweet thing to say, but Rick couldn't possibly know that. "A small part of me had hoped that Dad would show up today."

Rick parked the vehicle and pressed his spare key to the house into her palm. As their hands connected the temperature inside the vehicle rose. He held on a little longer than necessary.

She tugged at her jacket collar. A fluttery feeling tumbled through her stomach. "Thanks for the ride." It came out all breathy and soft.

Rick opened and closed his mouth as if struggling for his words. "I'm staying in the kennel, remember? I was coming back here anyway."

She turned away. A sudden coolness hit her core. Rick's attention was loyalty to Frankie, not to her. He was doing his job. He was protecting a citizen of Chenaniah River. He was not her boyfriend, not even a casual friend. He was a cop. Everything fell second to that.

"I'll walk you to the door to make sure everything is okay." His words confirmed her thoughts.

They dashed from the car to the protection of the front porch. The rain was coming down hard. Only in southern Ontario could you have knee-deep snow one week and freezing rain transform it into mud the next.

Jessie bounded up the steps to reach the cover of the porch. She stopped short. Rick bumped into her back.

The front door hung barely open. Rick stepped around her, settled both hands on her shoulders, and moved her aside. He dipped his head and peered directly into her eyes. "Stay here." He waited until she nodded before he forced the door the rest of the way and disappeared into the house.

She tiptoed to the door and peeked inside. Her purse lay open on the floor with half the contents spilled out. Her heartbeat thudded in her ears. Every creak and groan in the house instantly intensified. Her purse *was* with her at the funeral. She'd known it. Someone had taken, it and then broken into her house.

Ignoring Rick's instructions, she dashed in and scooped up her purse. She intended to go right back outside and wait where Rick told her to, but the immediate area seemed undisturbed. Maybe no one was here? Could she have left her purse at home? She rubbed her temple in a circular motion. It'd been a long day. She didn't know what to think anymore.

She tiptoed into the kitchen. Everything looked fine here, too. Some of the tension left her body until a familiar creak on the old wooden floor sounded from behind. She went rigid. Grabbing a cooking pot, the closest available weapon, she spun with all her might

Rick ducked, caught her arm, and twisted her around. He yanked her back against his chest. "I told you to wait on the porch." His warm breath tickled her ear with each hard exhalation, and his day-old stubble scratched her cheek. His chest heaved against her back.

"My purse is here," she whispered. "I knew I had it with me at the funeral."

A floorboard creaked above them. She instinctively tipped her head back to look at the ceiling and hit the top of her head on Rick's chin. He spun her around until they stood nose to nose. He pressed a finger to her lips and spoke low, "Go outside and get Max from the kennel." He gave her a nudge toward the back door and drew his gun.

She couldn't take her eyes off the weapon.

He cupped her chin and forced her to look into his eyes. "It's going to be okay. Go get Max."

A tear built in the corner of her eye. She wasn't going to cry. Not now. She'd made it through the entire day without crying. She would not break down now. She blinked hard, but it trickled down her cheek anyway.

He rubbed it away with the pad of his thumb. "Trust me?"

She nodded. She dashed out the back door and flattened her back against the white vinyl siding that butted against the boarded-up kitchen window. Her heart throbbed in her chest. She panted to catch her breath. Max. She had to get Max.

She sprinted to the kennel and put Max on a lead, suddenly grateful for the hours Rick had spent shifting Max's loyalty to her. She confidently took command of him. They stood in the open doorway of the kennel. Max looked at her, waiting for direction. She stared at the open back door to the house.

What if Rick never came back? What if something happened to him? What if the intruder was outside now, watching her, waiting for Rick to leave her vulnerable? She tightened her grip on Max's leash.

The yard felt eerily quiet with only the sound of the freezing rain pinging off the roof shingles. In the tree line, a face flashed. She squinted. Was it a face? Were her trumped-up emotions messing with her head?

Max growled and confirmed her suspicions. She unclipped his leash. "Get him, Max!"

Thrashing sounds of a body forging a new path through the back trails joined the sounds of rain. Jessie spun back toward the house and hesitated. Should she go back into the kennel alone or return to the house and tell Rick the intruder was out here? What if there was more than one intruder? There was more than one person that night she was pushed into the river. Nope. Alone in the kennel wasn't an option.

She crept back into the kitchen. Footsteps moved through the rooms above her. *Please Lord, let it be Rick.* She edged her way around the island and grabbed a large knife from the butcher block as she passed. The refrigerator hummed. The clock's minute hand ticked. Her heavy breathing echoed through her ears. She inched her way around a corner, knife first.

A sudden force slammed down on her forearms.

She screamed.

The blade clattered to the floor. Her arms were pinned behind her back. She stomped down as hard as she could on the foot of her captor.

"Why can't you listen to me?" Rick roared in pain as he loosened his grip on her. "I could have hurt you!" His eyes shone, locking on her face. His nostrils flared.

She sagged against the wall. "Someone was outside. Max went after him." Footsteps pounded down the stairs.

Jessie jumped as Rick faced the noise, the gun from his waistband again in his hand.

The front door banged against the house as a hooded man, dressed all in black, sprinted toward the tree line and disappeared into the woods.

Rick turned and dropped his gaze to hers. "Someone was here, too."

"Thanks, Aunt Norma." Rick pulled his aunt into an exuberant hug that shook loose a few wispy strands of gray from the bun gathered at the nape of her neck.

"Oh, it's nothing." Aunt Norma looked over Rick's shoulder and fixed her attention on Jessie, checking her out from top to bottom.

Jessie nervously straightened her jacket and ran a hand through her hair. Aunt Norma's look of approval eased the knot in her stomach.

"I don't want to intrude," Jessie said.

Aunt Norma stopped her with a wave of the hand. "It's fine. Besides, I invited you for a visit."

"Yes, but—"

"And you're the first young lady my Rick has brought home in years," she continued as if Jessie hadn't spoken.

Heat climbed Jessie's neck at the insinuation that she was Rick's young lady. If Rick was labelling her, it was more likely he'd call her his disobedient charge than his lady.

Rick had declared Frankie's house a crime scene and insisted she leave for her safety. She considered calling Steadman, but she didn't have the energy to rehash everything that happened. Not yet.

Rick laughed at Aunt Norma's comment about her being his girl. He nudged Jessie and gestured for her to give him her coat.

She shrugged out of her jacket. Why didn't he correct Norma?

"It should only be the one night," Rick said as he hung up her coat on the hook by the door. "I need to do a bit of investigative work before I consider it safe enough for her to return home. The chief was in the area when I called in the disturbance, so he's there now securing the scene."

"Of course, dear." Aunt Norma threaded her arm through Jessie's and steered her from the foyer into the living room. "We'll be okay. We'll get reacquainted."

Jessie looked over her shoulder at Rick. His intense stare seemed to ask the same question flooding Jessie's mind. What if she brought trouble to Aunt Norma's doorstep?

"I'll be back as soon as I can," Rick promised. He waited until she nodded before he left.

"Do you drink tea, dear?" Aunt Norma's grandmotherly instincts took over as soon as the front door closed.

"Oh, I don't want to be a bother."

"It's no bother at all. I'll run to the kitchen and put the kettle on to boil. Make yourself comfortable." She gave Jessie's shoulder a squeeze and headed into the kitchen.

Jessie looked around. Where exactly should she make herself comfortable? The fireplace mantle, end tables, and all visible surfaces displayed layers of framed pictures. The frames in the front partially blocked the frames behind. Every wall space flaunted a portrait, cross stitch, or animal poster with a Scripture verse. Both the sofa and the armchair held partially finished knitting projects of baby booties and hats, and a small pile of Bible study books towered precariously on the footstool near an open Bible.

Jessie carefully relocated a partially knitted hat from the sofa onto the coffee table to make space for her to sit. Under the coffee table were stacks and stacks of photo albums.

"Is herbal tea okay or do you prefer black tea?" Aunt Norma called from the kitchen where a kettle began to whistle.

"Either is fine. I'll have whatever you are having." Jessie picked up an album and flipped it open. Inside were clippings of newspaper articles about Rick's career as an officer. At first, they were all commendations, but the headlines changed and grew increasingly negative. Jessie flipped a few more pages, scanning the text. She didn't recognize the reporter's name, Ronald Anderson.

The teacups rattled on their saucers as Aunt Norma carried them, a silver teapot, and cream and sugar containers on a matching silver tray. "Oh dear, I have no place to set this."

Jessie neatly stacked the scattered magazines, noticing one for which she regularly freelanced in the mix. "Is this a good place?"

"Yes, thank you. I guess my housekeeping skills have been lax." She set the tray down. "I remember when I thought retiring from teaching would free my schedule, but I'm busier than ever." She noticed the album Jessie held and frowned.

"Should I have not looked at this?" Jessie tucked the clippings away and closed the book.

"It's Rick's story to tell." Aunt Norma poured tea into the two cups, handing Jessie one. "You can doctor this up however you like."

"Why did Rick return to Chenaniah River?" Jessie stirred in some sugar and a splash of milk and relaxed into the sofa.

"Lousy reporting," Aunt Norma said. She took the album from Jessie's lap. "That journalist was looking for his fifteen minutes of fame, and he got it by sensationalizing a tragedy at Rick's expense."

Jessie's gut churned. Even lousy reporting contained a kernel of truth.

"Have a cookie." Aunt Norma nudged the tray closer to Jessie.

She obediently took one. "You and Rick must be close."

"Ever since his mom died. I've tried to fill that void as much as I can. It was harder when he lived in the city, but now that he's home again..." Her voice trailed off. It was odd that she considered Chenaniah River to be Rick's home even though his family had lived the same number of years out of province.

Jessie sipped her tea. Comforting warmth coated her throat and flooded her insides. "Is that a flyer for the diamond hunt?" She gestured to a poster on the end table.

"Yes, I promised the mayor I'd put it up in the church." Aunt Norma clucked her tongue. "Do you have your ticket yet?"

Jessie smiled. She bought her ticket the day her editor accepted her story pitch about the town festivities. "Of course. It wouldn't be a winter in Chenaniah River without hunting for that elusive diamond." Jessie munched on her cookie. "Although I haven't started searching yet."

"Who's your date for the Valentine's Ball?" Aunt Norma looked at her over the rim of her teacup. Something about the way she asked the question made Jessie suspect Aunt Norma already had a date in mind for Jessie.

Jessie fidgeted with the sugar spoon resting on the saucer. Her cheeks felt impossibly hot. "I haven't got a date. I'm reporting on the event, so technically, I'll be working."

"Pish-posh." Norma waved away Jessie's objections. "No reason you can't mix business with pleasure. I know a young man who makes a handsome escort."

Jessie picked up a magazine and started flipping through the pages to avoid meeting Aunt Norma's eyes and her not so subtle suggestion.

"Find something interesting in there?" Aunt Norma smiled innocently.

"Ah, this is neat," Jessie opened to a page featuring a charming picture of a country home under the title: *Secret Rooms in Old Farmhouses. Could Your Homestead Have One?*

Aunt Norma glanced at the spread. "That was an

interesting article. You know, with this town's bootlegging history, I wouldn't be surprised if there was an entire underground tunnel system connecting the key homes from that era. Wouldn't surprise me one bit."

Could Frankie's place have a secret room? Considering their house was the original home of Grandpa James and Grandma Maggie, there was a good chance. Or better yet, could there be a room that led to a series of underground tunnels? Is that why someone broke into the house tonight? Well, maybe even the other night? Maybe it was the same people who hadn't found what they were looking for the first time? "Do you mind if I keep this?"

"Sure," Aunt Norma flapped her hand at the magazine. "Keep it for as long as you want."

Jessie mind spun with possibilities. Secret rooms, underground tunnels, lost diamonds, and missing drugs. Her editor might get a bigger story than she expected.

Chapter 11

"Are you ready to go home?" Rick asked Jessie the next day.

"All ready." Jessie had been ready since the sun came up and warmed the tips of grass poking through the frosty ground. But there was no sense in poking the bear. Rick's sour tone and tight features commanded compliance, not complaints.

She turned to Aunt Norma. "Thanks for having me while Rick took care of things at the house, and thank you for the wonderful dinner last night and lunch today."

Aunt Norma pulled her into a grandmotherly embrace. "Anytime, dear. I hope you were able to get some work done."

She did as much research for her article as she could, tracking down the names of previous diamond hunt winners and old articles about them. A few of the local winners were still around. She hoped for the chance to speak with some of them. They could be great interviews that provided sidebar information.

She studied Rick's profile from the passenger seat as he backed his car out of the driveway. He'd already verbalized his preference that she maintain a low profile until he figured out what was going on, but she didn't pass on her Africa assignment to shut herself up in the house. Now that she had decided to remain in Chenaniah River, she had to make good on her promise of a great article about a local in-country getaway. To do that, she needed to get out onto the streets. She fiddled with her purse strap in her lap. "How do you feel about a little diamond hunting?"

"You bought a ticket to the hunt?" The corners of his lips shifted from the perpetual frown he had worn since picking her up. He had a great smile.

"Of course, I did. Didn't you?" She took out the loaner phone Rick had given to her when her phone went into the river. She swiped open the app that used GPS tracking to guide hunters to various clues hidden all over the town. A diamond icon popped up on her screen, and a vibrating pickaxe broke it apart. A "note" scrolled open revealing their first clue. She waggled her phone in front of him. "You want to hunt diamonds?"

A full smile split his face, and her insides warmed. He pointed the car toward the downtown and gave her his full attention. "Let's do this."

She read the clue aloud. "Use all of your smell powers and find something with the scent of flowers."

"Flowers in the middle of winter," Rick mused. He pushed against the steering wheel to straighten his arms and leaned back against the driver's seat. His lips puckered in concentration.

"It can't be outside." Jessie mentally scrolled through all the flower places in Chenaniah River. "I know!" She snapped her fingers. "Always Spring – the florist on the main street. It has to be it. The first one is always easy."

A glint flickered in his eyes. "How do you know the first clue is always easy? You haven't done this for years." He tossed her a sassy grin as he parked the car in the parking lot.

She punched his arm. "It has to be easy, or none of the tourists could play. Come on, let's go." She got out of the car and tromped toward Always Spring.

A handful of tourists led by their phone screens confirmed her guess. The next clue had to be near the store. She turned to check and see if Rick followed. The wind caught her hair, and it billowed all around her face. She gathered the strands in one hand and held it back while she waited for him to catch up.

"I'll race you!" He bolted ahead of her and yanked open the store's door, sending a strand of bells hanging on a ribbon jingling.

"That's not fair!" She grabbed hold of his arm, and they tumbled inside like a pair of entangled teenagers. He started laughing again, and she leaned into him. Was she flirting? For once, she didn't want to overthink it.

Holding out her phone to lead the way, they followed the thumping diamond icon until it stopped pulsing. Jessie lifted her nose and sniffed the scented air. "How do we find the one flower with the clue?"

"There has to be something on the app that narrows down the search." Rick took the phone from her and turned on the camera feature. He held it in front of them and scanned the store. "There!" He pointed to the back corner. "There's an animated diamond behind the potted tulips."

He zoomed in on the diamond, and it twirled as the GPS sensor logged in their location. It lifted off the ground and cracked open to reveal another scroll. Jessie clicked it, and it rolled open. "You won't need to wear your sweater when you're here to get your letter. Find me and win a chance to play again tomorrow." She pursed her lips.

She spun to the clerk. "The post office?"

He shrugged. "If I told you, they'd take my store off the list of diamond stops. You have to figure it out on your own."

"It has to be." Rick tugged her back onto the street. "Jessie!"

They both turned around at Steadman's voice. He schmoozed with some tourists outside the store, shook their hands, and then excused himself to join Jessie and Rick.

"Hi, Steadman." She fell against Rick, shoulder to shoulder, breathing heavily.

"Diamond hunting?" Steadman's eyes twinkled. He nodded at Rick.

"Isn't everyone?" Rick's laugh warmed Jessie's insides. For the first time since she arrived, he looked like he was having fun. He looked a bit more like the boy she remembered. She was glad that she was a part of his good mood.

"I hope they are all diamond hunting." Steadman scanned the bustling crowd. "How are you, Jessie? Beth has been worried."

"I'm okay." She brushed off his concern, sobering up at his reminder of all that had recently transpired.

"Could you stop in later and reassure her? After losing Frankie, she is in full mama bear mode. I don't think she'll relax until we get a postcard from your next travel destination."

She ignored the dig about leaving, although it was nice to be worried over. "Of course, I'll stop in."

"I'll bring her by later," Rick promised.

"And may I ask what happened at the funeral that sent you running out, Officer Chandler?"

"Sorry, sir. I can't comment on an ongoing investigation."

"I'm not asking as the mayor," he scoffed, "but as Jessie's cousin. Someone is targeting my family. I'd like to know why."

Jessie tensed. "If this is family related, could Steadman be in danger, too?" She spun toward Steadman. "Do you have any allergies?"

"I'll be fine," he assured her.

"If this was about the mayor, he'd already know," Rick said.

"And no," Steadman added, "I have no allergies."

"That's right. You and Frankie inherited your sensitivities through your father's side of the family," Rick said.

"How did you know that?" Steadman fixed his gaze on Rick.

How did he know that? Jessie cocked her head and waited for his answer.

"I grew up with them, remember?"

Steadman narrowed his eyes and studied him for a minute longer before turning his attention back to Jessie. His features softened as his gaze found hers. "Enjoy the hunt, sweetheart. Good luck!"

Rick and Jessie left Steadman to his socializing and jogged across the street to the drugstore that housed a tiny post office. They stood on the sidewalk and pointed the phone at everything, but no icon popped up.

"Maybe we got it wrong." Rick furrowed his brow.

Jessie scanned the exterior of the store. "Maybe it's not a regular letter. Maybe it's like a letter to the editor. Like in a newspaper?"

They went inside to the newspaper stand near the cashier. Jessie scanned the front pages of the papers. Ronald Anderson's byline caught her attention.

"Find something?" Rick popped his head out from behind the magazine rack that he was scanning.

She held up the newspaper. "Did you see this?"

His eyes darkened, and he tightened his lips.

Jessie speed-read the newest article bashing Rick. "How does Anderson know what's going on here? Why does he say that I should consider what happened to the last woman under your protection?"

Rick's chin jutted out and his face flushed. "This guy has a reputation for not gathering all the details before going to press."

"From the sound of this, I don't have all the details either." Nearby shoppers cast a few curious looks their way. She lowered her voice. "What aren't you telling me?"

He didn't answer.

She took the paper to the cashier and paid for it. She looked back at him. He stood right where she'd left him in front of the magazines. "Coming?"

They walked in silence to his car. All the joy had been sucked out their afternoon.

Rick didn't make a sound as she read the entire article in the front passenger seat of his car. She snuck glances his way. His eyes stayed closed, and his Adam's apple bobbed. Was he praying?

"This Anderson guy, he's not a fan?" She folded the paper on her lap.

"To say the least."

His thickening voice melted the barriers around her heart. When she combined this information with her earlier conversation with Aunt Norma, it was easy to piece things together. "Your informant called you and told you she thought she was compromised, but you failed to extract her." She held his gaze. "Is that correct?"

"Only partially," Rick bristled. "This informant thrived on drama. She insisted she was in immediate danger every time she called. She pulled me off important cases. She pulled me away from people who needed my help. Then, I'd learn that she'd exaggerated her distress. She was a lonely woman."

Jessie had heard of this happening between informants and cops. Even though she didn't write hard-hitting journalism, she still attended some of the same conferences and workshops as many other writers.

"When she called this time," Rick continued, "I was in the middle of a domestic dispute. I couldn't just leave the mother and little girl depending on me. So, I made a judgment call that I'll regret for the rest of my life," his voice cracked.

"Because she wasn't crying wolf," Jessie finished softly.

"She was dead by the time I got there." His vacant stare stabbed her heart.

"How come none of the articles mention the woman and her daughter?" Anderson's shoddy reporting filled her mouth with bitterness. He made no mention of the extenuating circumstances that contributed to Rick's decision.

"If I disclosed their identity, Anderson would exploit them, and the woman's husband would be able to find her."

Her chest swelled. Rick wouldn't give their names, not even to save his own. Her voice dipped. "It sounds like you saved their lives."

He looked away. "But at what cost?"

He spoke so softly that she almost didn't hear his words. Anderson's blatant abuse of the press sent a roiling heat through her belly. It was easy to manipulate public opinion and ruin a life, and too many reporters did it to up their ratings. She slapped the paper against her thighs. "This isn't right."

Rick's eyes widened at her sharp tone. "There is nothing I can do but take the hits." His expression held none of the bitterness she expected to see.

She reached over and took his hand in hers. She weaved her gloved fingers with his and gave his hand a gentle squeeze.

He looked down at their entwined hands and relief washed over his face, but only for a minute. He cleared his throat. "We have a diamond to find. If this post office is wrong, maybe the main post office is right." He tugged his hand free and started the engine.

She shoved her disappointment down. This was about him, not her. And if he didn't want to talk about it anymore, if he didn't welcome her offer of comfort, she wasn't going to press him.

"Aren't they renovating the main post office?" There were construction trucks outside the post office yesterday, and the sidewalks on either side of the front door blocked off with caution tape.

"Yes, and just inside the front doors are heat vents that blast you as you walk in. The clue said we wouldn't need a sweater."

"That's got to be it."

Rick eased the vehicle into traffic and five minutes later parked on the street across from the main post office.

"Jessie?"

"Yeah?" Jessie's hand rested on the door handle. She looked back at Rick.

"Thanks."

He didn't say anything else. He didn't have to. She knew what it was to work through the stages of grief. He needed space to feel whatever emotions were raging inside. She could give him that.

Soon, they huddled in the lobby of the main post office, and another diamond cracked open. They'd won the chance to participate in Level Two tomorrow and search again.

Rick's eyes sparkled as they did back when they were teens, and her heart surged to have been a small part of replacing the sadness that had lingered there while she had read the news article.

They walked back outside, and she nudged him with her shoulder. "Remember the last hunt we did together?" On a day reminiscent of today, they had stood toe-to-toe, euphoric for finding the daily clues. Rick had brushed her hair back from her face, stroked her cheek, and tugged her close. He had leaned in like he was going to kiss her, and she had closed her eyes in anticipation. But at the last minute, he had bypassed her lips and pressed his mouth against her forehead. Her skin tingled at the memory.

"Yeah, I do." Rick stopped. He lifted his hand like a replay from the past.

She froze.

He tucked a strand of hair around her ear and the back of his hand grazed her cheekbone and chin.

She instinctively leaned into him, and he rotated his wrist and cradled her cheek. Tingling zinged all the way down to her toes. No matter what Anderson wrote, this was an honorable man. She was sure of it. She swayed forward until their bodies were mere millimeters apart.

He slipped his hand around the back of her neck and tangled his fingers in her hair, tugging her gently. She read the question in his eyes, and she let him pull her even closer. He rubbed his thumb across her lips, and she wet them. Her heart thudded. He wasn't going to bypass her mouth this time. She prayed that he wouldn't.

A gunshot split the stillness.

Rick yanked Jessie down behind a mailbox. A second bullet embedded in the pavement near their feet.

Jessie automatically recoiled from the point of impact, and Rick forcibly pulled her back down and shoved her head closer to the ground.

Chaos and screams abounded. Shoppers and diamond hunters scattered, dropping packages, purses, and phones.

An eerie silence settled over them. Was it over? A third shot zinged over their heads. Jessie trembled so violently that Rick ran his hands up and down her arms as if checking for injuries. "I'm okay," she said. "I'm okay."

He peered around the corner of their hiding spot. A fourth bullet zipped past, narrowly missing him. He jerked back. He pressed against the mailbox and wrapped her in his arms.

She buried her face in his chest. A tremor ripped through her. Did the shooter have bad aim? Was it another warning? How many warnings would she get?

A distant siren sounded, getting louder by the second.

Someone had phoned the police. She peeked over Rick's shoulder. All was quiet. Rick tightened his arms around her. He rubbed his hands up and down her trembling back. "It's going to be okay. It's going to be okay," he kept repeating.

But she wasn't sure she believed it anymore.

Chapter 12

Rick finished off his third cup of coffee. It was already 8:00 a.m., and he wasn't any closer to solving this thing than he was at 6:00 a.m. when he'd arrived at the police station. How was the shooter connected to Jessie? Was it all tied to the drug ring? Was this about her dad's supposed pension theft? Were the local police dirty? Who could he trust? He rubbed at the knots in the back of his neck. He needed more coffee to function.

It didn't help that he'd spent over an hour last night with Pete trying to calm Jack down. Jack threatened to leave their protective custody if anything else happened to Jessie. He'd made some snarky comment about Rick's inability to keep the women under his care safe. Another dig about Sarah.

"The bullet casings match those found at Jessie's last week." Gavin stood at the side of his desk. "Thought you'd want to know." Gavin had been the responding officer to the shooting and had stayed late yesterday to process the scene. "I'm canvassing the hunting community to see if anyone of interest was hunting in the area on both dates." Gavin went to his desk, which sat diagonally across from Rick's.

"Keep me posted." The shooter was getting brazen, shooting in the daylight.

Gavin nodded.

"Tough morning?" Daniel set a fresh coffee on the corner of Rick's desk and handed a laptop to him before shrugging out of his jacket.

"More like a tough week. Some good news would turn it around." Rick took a long drink of the coffee, sat back, and sighed. "Thanks."

Daniel smiled. "Frankie's computer showed mostly searches on ancestry websites. It looked like Frankie was tracing his family tree. It also showed some digging into the sale of Eastmore."

Rick shook his head. He had hoped Daniel's expertise in computers would reveal something more. Instead, it added more questions. Why was Frankie searching his ancestry? Was it connected, or was it a hobby?

"The factory? That's odd." Gavin looked up from the reports he was filling out about yesterday's shooting.

"It is," Rick agreed. What could be interesting about

the factory all these years after it had closed?

"One more thing." Daniel leaned against Rick's desk. "A phone was turned in last night. Guess who it belongs to?"

Rick arched a brow.

"Jessie Berns."

Rick bolted upright in his chair. Hot coffee sloshed over the rim and burned his hand. "And you didn't lead with that! Can you recover anything?"

Daniel laughed. "Already working on it. It's damaged from being in the river, but I'm hopeful."

"Rick, in my office." The command sounded from across the room. Chief Brewer glared from his doorway. He didn't wait for Rick to respond. He turned and stormed inside his office.

Daniel's eyes widened. "Good luck, man."

Rick closed his computer. No one would meet his eyes as he crossed the room. He leaned a shoulder against the doorframe of Brewer's office. "Yeah, Chief?"

"Shut the door and take a seat."

Rick obeyed.

"How's the investigation into Jessie Berns going?" Conrad's brows pinched together over a brooding stare. It wasn't a look of concern.

"Jessie's phone turned up. Daniel is trying to recover what he can."

Conrad silently tapped his fingertips together. It set Rick on edge.

"And the phone is here, in evidence?" The chief's eyes remained unreadable.

"Daniel is working on it now."

"Can you explain this?" Conrad moved a photograph across the desk toward Rick.

Rick picked up a glossy 8x10 of him and Pete in the hospital waiting room. Someone took it the night Jessie fell through the ice. He didn't understand.

He looked up at the chief.

Nothing.

He looked back at the photograph.

"How about this one?" Conrad slid another picture across the desk. This one zoomed in on Rick handing a thumb drive to Pete—the thumb drive that Conrad had told him to log into evidence, but Pete asked him to sit on.

Rick tossed the pictures back onto the desk. "That's a friend and me at the hospital waiting for news on Jessie." His mind spun. Who was in the waiting room that night? Why would they take this picture? What had the chief so riled up?

Conrad's red complexion deepened. "I can see you're with a friend, and the date stamp is the night someone attacked Ms. Berns. Gavin suggested we look into the security footage from the hospital's cameras in case whoever had targeted Jessie circled back."

No one had mentioned that to Rick.

"What are you handing to your friend?" The chief's tone suggested he already knew what it was, and Rick got the feeling the question was merely a formality.

"A USB, why?" Rick stalled. What was Conrad's goal?

"Here's what I think is happening. Your old friend returns to town and finds herself in the same trouble that sank her brother. Out of a sense of obligation to her brother, you help her out, but she ends up in trouble again."

Rick opened his mouth.

"And again," Conrad cut him off and stood up.

"But—"

"You're so caught up in your memories of the good ol' days with Frankie and Jessie, that you don't see she could tank your career and make a mockery of this office." Conrad paced behind his desk.

"That's not—"

Conrad leaned onto his fisted hands, angling across the desk as far as his six-foot frame could reach. "And now you've failed to log in evidence. You have given police information to a person of interest, and despite being the first responder to every emergency Ms. Berns experiences, you're no closer to eliminating the threat against her."

"That's because—"

Conrad cut through the air with a downward slash. His continual talking over Rick was a well-known interrogation tactic. But why was the man interrogating him?

"If another woman dies on your watch, you're history."

Rick's insides heaved. "This has nothing to do with Sarah."

"It has everything to do with Sarah," Conrad bellowed.

If the guys outside didn't know what was going on before, they sure knew now.

"When the mayor calls me personally and tells me that tourists are following the stories in the paper and stopping him on the street—"

"Stories in the newspaper?" So, the chief had seen it, too. His past had finally collided with his present.

"Doubts about your abilities as an officer have been expressed."

Rick tensed. "Jessie Berns is alive because of me."

Conrad raised an unimpressed eyebrow. "For how long?"

"I don't have to sit here and listen to this. Family or not, the mayor has no business sticking his nose—" Rick thrust his chair backward and started to stand.

"Sit down!" Conrad thundered. He waited until Rick obeyed. "The mayor is well within his rights to inquire about an investigation when it portrays Chenaniah River as a potentially unsafe destination, especially considering yesterday's shooting is now all over the news. 'The consequences of a small-town police department filling its vacancy with a reject from the bigger city might prove deadly,'" Conrad quoted. "That's the headline story online right now."

Anderson's words drove a spike of uncertainty into Rick's chest. What if he couldn't stop whatever was coming? What if he wasn't able to save Jessie? He forced his doubts aside. "That's hardly reporting. Anderson should be writing for tabloids."

"That's not the kind of publicity the Winter Diamond Festival needs."

"No, sir."

He nudged the picture closer to Rick again. "That USB looks a lot like the one missing from evidence. You know, the one with the parking lot security footage from the night someone attacked Ms. Berns." The way the chief spoke the word 'missing' left no doubt he questioned Rick's story.

"I haven't logged the USB into evidence yet." Why had Conrad looked for the thumb drive? It's hardly a task the chief would pursue unless he had a personal interest in the case.

The chief was there the night Jessie arrived. His fingerprints were on the pill bottle. Would Frankie have addressed the chief as *officer*, as Jack had heard?

"Do you need a reminder about our policy regarding the logging of evidence?" Conrad asked.

"You made a show of calling me in here. If you've got something to say, then come right out and say it." Rick remained seated, but not out of respect. He needed Conrad to think he got the better of him. Rick wanted Conrad overconfident. Maybe then, he'd get a glimpse of which side of the law he worked on.

"Alright. I don't trust you." Conrad folded his arms across his chest.

Right back at ya.

"All this started when Ms. Berns came to town."

Don't I know it.

"I'm watching you, Rick."

"You're not the only one." Rick nodded to the picture.

The chief nodded. "That's all for now. Watch your step."

Rick left the office, and the workroom buzzed to life. So much for the privacy offered by a closed door. He stomped over to the evidence locker and started the paperwork to log in the thumb drive.

"Rick," Daniel called from his desk. "None of the pictures on Jessie's phone are clear enough to be helpful. The best shot is blurred. She likely snapped it when she was shoved. I'll keep working on it."

"Who brought the phone in?"

"Mayor Munroe. Said some kid gave it to his wife on the street. He turned it on and recognized it was Jessie's and brought it right here."

As Daniel spoke, Jessie's phone vibrated on his desk. A text came in from an unknown number. Daniel picked it up and read out loud, *Get to Chenaniah Manor!*

Daniel arched a brow. "What's at Chenaniah Manor?"

The bottom dropped out of Rick's stomach. "Jessie."

Convincing Rick to let her keep her appointment at Chenaniah Manor had been a hard sell, considering everything that happened yesterday. But Jessie had a deadline to meet, and she didn't have time to sit around the police station all day. She had provided Rick with her itinerary and agreed to check in with him at set times. She prayed that would be enough to keep her safe.

Expensive paintings decorated Chenaniah Manor's bright walls. Plush carpet cushioned Jessie's steps as only high-end carpet could. Many of the seniors living at Chenaniah Manor had been part of the core group that banded together to re-launch Chenaniah River as a tourist destination. Jessie had been under the impression this group had been the hardest hit financially, all of them losing their company pensions in the bankruptcy.

She poked her head into the atrium. A lush garden-like sunroom filled a central octagon space on the main floor. Greenery grew over the balconies on the first two stories. The balconies on the top level were unfinished. Some still had a two by four as a railing rather than the wrought iron and clear glass used on the lower levels. It all seemed expensive for seniors on a fixed income.

"You must be Jessie. Welcome." A portly man shuffled around the welcome desk, extending a hand. "I'm Derek Bommel, owner of Chenaniah Manor. My brother, Sam, owns Sam's Animal Training. He introduced us at Frankie's funeral, but I don't expect you to remember me."

She allowed Derek's meaty grip to engulf hers, and he eagerly pumped her hand. It left her with an urge to wipe her palm on her slacks.

"Thank you for allowing me to interview some of your residents."

He waved off her thanks. "I simply made your request known and the residents responded on their own. Chenaniah Manor is their home, and they have complete freedom to take part in activities we arrange or to opt out." He led her through double glass doors. "I cleared a spot for you in the atrium. This is a favorite space for many of our residents. May I ask why you are interested in our seniors?"

She set her bag on the floor by a chair and pulled out

her laptop. "They can provide backstory for my article on the Winter Diamond Festival. Those who lost their jobs when Eastmore closed had key roles in reinventing the town. Backstory doesn't always make the article, but it helps frame the final product with accuracy and integrity." Something that hack reporter, Anderson, needed to learn.

Derek nodded along as she spoke. "I see. I'll fetch Stan Broadwick. He's the only one available for today, but others showed interest and are willing to meet you on another day."

Derek hurried out, and she shaded her eyes. It was easy to see why residents would favor this space in the dreary winter months. An elderly gentleman shuffled by aided by a young man. She smiled at them.

The young man's lips twitched. For the briefest second his face contorted into a hateful glare that sucked the air from her lungs, but he replaced it with indifference so quickly that she wondered if she imagined it.

The duo exited from a side door as Mr. Broadwick lumbered into the room with beige pants hiked up to his chest. A cane balanced him as he hobbled along. She forced the unpleasant exchange with the stranger from her mind, but Mr. Broadwick picked up on her anxiety.

"Don't worry about old Pat." He nodded at the retreating pair. "His wife just died. It's been difficult."

"Who's the man helping him?"

"His son, Rob."

She extended her hand, still trying to shake off Rob's anger. "I appreciate you taking the time to speak to me, Mr. Broadwick."

He shook her hand and *humphed*, before sitting down. "Might as well, not like my ungrateful kids ever come. You're the first person to visit me all month."

Her heart twanged at the way he covered up loneliness with abruptness. He'd be an excellent candidate for dog therapy. Maybe she'd mention it to Sam and see if she could get Mr. Broadwick on his therapy list.

She flipped open her notebook. "I have a few questions about what Chenaniah River was like back when the Eastmore plant closed. Can you tell me about life back then?" She could have filled this portion of the story with her memories from life in that time, but objective reporters did not insert themselves into the story.

"Life was great until our union rep steered us wrong." He shifted in his seat and pinched his eyes into a squint.

"What do you mean?" Closed doors provided them with a sense of privacy despite the clanging noises that drifted in from work on a nearby balcony.

"Eastmore offered us a contract, but our representative urged us to hold out for a better deal. Said Eastmore was bluffing about this being their best and final offer. That rep convinced the younger crew, the hotheads, to reject the offer." He rubbed his right knee.

"The hotheads?"

"You know, the guys they always show on the news during this kind of stuff. Those yahoos were running their mouths with more foolish talk than good." He adjusted himself again and grimaced.

She paused in her note taking. "Are you okay? You seem to be in pain."

"I'm fine. Just my bum knee is giving me grief." He rotated his hand over his knee in a circular motion. "Eastmore did exactly what they said they would do if we rejected the offer. They closed." Sweat droplets beaded up on his forehead. He pulled a fabric square out of his pocket and dabbed at them.

"How many years did you work there?"

"Forty-two, and I didn't see a penny of my pension."

She winced. Did Stan know who she was?

"Relax. I know you're Jack's daughter. We all know. Despite what some of the others think, I don't believe the crimes of a father should follow his children." He stuffed the handkerchief into his shirt pocket. He huffed and shifted again.

Palpable relief washed over her. She touched a hand to Stan's arm. "That means a lot to me."

He flinched again.

"Can I call someone for you? You seem very

uncomfortable."

"I'll be okay. Just had surgery on my knee, and it still hurts."

"Are you due for some more pain meds?"

"Naw, they don't help much."

"They should. If you're not getting relief, I can speak with the staff for you—"

"Leave it alone. It's fine." He removed his glasses and used the same pocket square to rub the lenses.

Why would he refuse pain meds when he was clearly in pain? The sounds of clanking on the third floor increased. She raised her voice. "This is a pretty nice place. How did you end up here?"

The door to the atrium burst open, and Rick rushed in a few steps ahead of a prattling Derek. "I'm sorry, Miss. Berns, but Officer Chandler insisted on seeing you right away."

A heavy feeling filled her stomach. What was he doing here? Why did he look so panicked?

"It's okay," she assured Derek. She turned to Mr. Broadwick. "Do you mind if Officer Chandler sits in for the rest of the interview? He's been helping me since I returned to town."

Mr. Broadwick's expression subtly hardened. "It's fine," he said. But it clearly wasn't.

She nodded at Rick to sit. She leaned closer to Stan.

"You were going to tell me how you ended up at Chenaniah Manor?"

Stan watched as Rick pulled up a chair and settled down beside her. "Most of us had planned to move in here but we could no longer afford it without our pension. Mr. Bommel gave us a special rate."

"That was kind," Rick said. She shot him a look that she hoped he would interpret as *keep quiet.*

"I suppose filling the rooms at a reduced cost was better than having the rooms empty." Jessie tapped a few notes into her computer.

"He even got the mayor to help, spinning some angle about taking care of our own." The clanking above them stopped, replaced by a scraping sound.

Rick studied the balconies.

What on earth were they doing on the third floor?

"Mayor Munroe's entire campaign revolved around Eastmore's closure and the ways he could transition Chenaniah River into a profitable town again," Stan said. "Munroe had a five-year plan to turn this place around. I was skeptical, but by golly, the man delivered." Mr. Broadwick slipped his glasses back onto his face. "That's better. Now I can see your pretty face."

She smiled and noted, *Ask Steadman about his campaign,* in her document. "Thank you, Mr. Broadwick. Can I call on you again if I need anything else?"

"Sure thing. I like the company." He heaved himself up, each movement accentuated with a grimace. Whoever was managing his pain meds wasn't doing a very good job.

Rick jumped up and offered his arm as assistance. Despite Stan's coolness toward Rick, he begrudgingly accepted his help.

She accompanied them to the door. Stan's hobbled gait moved at the pace of a snail. She exchanged a concerned look with Rick before she returned to the table to finish her notes. Rick remained in the doorway watching Stan Broadwick leave.

He turned and opened his mouth like he was going to say something, but he rushed her instead.

She half rose from her seat. "What's wro—"

Rick threw himself toward her.

A ceramic pot crashed to the ground and shattered. Rick shielded her, gun pointed upward, scanning the balconies for movement.

She pushed herself up. All the balconies had two-by-fours as railings except for one—the one directly above her.

Chapter 13

If he hadn't lingered by the door to watch Stan leave, he might not have seen the pot pushed to the edge of the balcony. Rick didn't feel proud of the last-minute rescue. He didn't feel heroic, although the female staff fawned over him like he was. His limbs shook, his chest ached, and a hard rock settled in his stomach... all symptoms of fear.

He scanned the crowd of medics, officers, staff, and residents. Things were moving quickly, almost too quickly to process. Someone in this crowd had tried to kill Jessie. That someone had nearly succeeded. Someone blended in so well that they had gone undetected. Knowing Jessie was potentially rubbing shoulders and accepting aid and condolences from the very person out to kill her, soured his gut. He'd come close to losing her again. Too close.

His muscles tensed as his roaming gaze landed on Jessie. She stood on the opposite side of Chenaniah

Manor's lobby and conversed with Chief Brewer. Her pale skin looked even more ashen in the harsh lights. She hugged her lean frame.

Rick lowered his voice so only Pete could hear the words he whispered into his phone. "She's fine," Rick assured him. He had called Pete as soon as the attention swarming him had died down. He stuffed his free hand into his coat pocket to cloak his clenching his fist. "She's shook up but fine."

"Why do you think the killer tipped his hand? If he wanted to hurt Jessie, he wouldn't have warned you first with that text message," Pete said.

"I know." Rick angled his body away from Jessie and the chief. "That bothers me too. This guy does everything for a reason."

"Don't let her out of your sight," Pete instructed.

"I won't." Rick clenched his jaw and disconnected the call. He slipped his phone into his pocket and focused his attention back on Jessie. He reached her side in a few long strides.

The chief excused himself as Rick approached.

Jessie gingerly touched her cheek where a soft blue bruise began to show. Rick covered her hand with his. "Are you okay?" He'd taken her down pretty hard.

"As good as you'd expect after that football tackle." She tugged her hand out from under his and wove her fingers together in front of her body, but she couldn't hide the way she trembled. Her eyes pleaded with him. "Tell me you've figured this out."

Everything inside of him wanted to assure her that he was one step ahead of this guy, but he couldn't lie to her. He couldn't say anything that might cause her to let down her guard. The potential danger wasn't worth the temporary relief. "Honestly, I'm barely keeping up. Whoever this is has been one step ahead of us the whole time."

She slumped.

Rick stuffed his hands into his front denim pockets. It took all his willpower to resist the temptation to gather her into his arms and assure her that she was safe.

"How did you know to come?" she asked.

"A text message came in on your old phone telling me to come to Chenaniah Manor."

She perked. "My old phone? The one that went into the river?"

"It was turned into the station. Whoever sent the message knew I had it. They obviously wanted me here."

She narrowed her eyes as she scanned the crowd milling about. "Why?"

He followed her gaze. "That's the million-dollar question. Who had your old phone number? Did Steadman and Beth?"

She twisted a strand of hair in her fingers. "Yes. My work had it. A few other travel writers. Frankie."

That didn't narrow things down. The murderer had Frankie's phone, which likely contained all the necessary contact information on Jessie.

An elderly gentleman slowly shuffled across the room. The way he glared at Jessie raised Rick's hackles, but he was too old and feeble to move a large ceramic pot.

Rick nudged her elbow. "You know him?"

She followed his gaze. "That's Pat," she said. "His wife just died."

Rick softened as the man collected his mail and returned to the elevator at a painful snail's pace. Some people got mad at the world when they were suffering.

Rick scanned the rest of the crowd. "Why did the killer warn me? I was lured here on purpose."

"Didn't you say that Frankie had been returning from Chenaniah Manor the day he died?"

"Yes, maybe—"

"Jessie!" Beth ran across the foyer and pulled Jessie into an embrace. She squeezed her and then pulled back to rake her gaze up and down Jessie's length as if looking for injuries. "What happened? I was out front when someone mentioned your name. I saw all the police cars and thought—I thought—" She tightened her hold on Jessie's arms before pulling her back into her arms for a second hug. "Are you hurt?" she whispered into Jessie's hair.

"I'm okay." Jessie smiled weakly and untangled herself from her aunt.

"Steadman is on his way." Beth slipped a protective arm around Jessie's waist and pulled her to her side, glaring at Rick as if everything was his fault.

Mamma Bear was out in full force.

Jessie tossed Rick a weak smile and subtly shrugged her shoulders. Theorizing was going to have to wait until Beth was convinced Jessie was fine.

The elevator dinged, and a handful of people exited: two senior citizens, a man about Rick's age, a gangly guy in his twenties, and Sam, the animal trainer that wanted to purchase Frankie's business.

Sam crossed the lobby with his dog obediently at his heels.

As Beth mothered Jessie with soothing sounds and back rubs, Rick rolled all the details over in his mind. The mayor turns in Jessie's phone. He and his wife are in the vicinity when she is targeted. The man who wants to buy Frankie's business is on site. Rick made a mental note to ask Gavin to check and see if Sam, the mayor, or Beth had ever hunted or had a license for the type of gun used to target Jessie.

Rick steered Jessie and Beth toward the atrium doors where the chief and others worked the scene.

Jessie leaned closer to Beth as she tried to take it all in. Rick's palms itched with a need to be the one consoling Jessie. He fisted his fingers at his side. His job was to protect, not console.

Jessie's gaze settled on the balcony with the missing railing. Her attention lingered there for a few uncomfortable seconds before turning to Chief Brewer. "Am I free to leave?"

Brewer looked up from his notepad. "Trouble seems to keep finding you, Ms. Berns. Are you sure you don't have any idea what's going on?"

Her eyes darkened. "I'm sure."

"Then you're free to go."

Rick stepped forward. "Sir, can I escort her home?" There was no way he was going to let her walk out those doors unprotected.

"No need for that. I will bring her home." Steadman swooped in and planted a kiss on Jessie's temple. Jessie nodded her approval at Rick.

"Then, I'll walk you out." Rick pressed his hand reassuringly into the small of her back and steered the small group toward the parking lot. The congested lobby parted like a crowd on a parade route making way for the performers and floats.

A bitter wind greeted them as the exit doors closed behind them. Rick scanned the parking lot for threats when his phone rang. Pete's name showed on the screen. "I need to take—"

A vehicle skidded to a stop at the bumper of his car. A man lurched from the driver's seat screaming, "I'm gonna kill you!"

Rick dropped his phone and shoved Jessie behind him.

Beth shrieked as Steadman yanked her to safety.

Rick absorbed a full front tackle and expertly flipped the assailant, pushing him face first against the side of the idling vehicle. Rick twisted the attacker's arms behind him and immobilized him with ease.

"What are you doing here?" Rick hissed in his ear.

"You said you'd keep her safe. You said that you'd protect her!" Spittle flew from Jack's mouth.

"I am. I did." Rick tightened his hold.

"Like you protected your last informant?"

Rick twisted Jack's arm harder until the fight drained from his body.

"That has nothing to do with—"

"Dad?" Jessie held Rick's phone to her ear. Pete was still yipping away.

"Jack?" Steadman took a threatening step toward his cousin.

"No." Rick's curt command stopped Steadman's advance, and Rick hustled Jack toward the back seat of the vehicle. He yanked the door open.

171

A murderous look filled the mayor's eyes.

Jessie followed Rick. "How long have you known?"

He had thought her complexion was colorless back in the manor after the attack. But the hue now shading her skin was so pallid it was almost translucent. Her hand held his phone a few inches from her ear and trembled. She no longer listened to Pete. Her attention was fixed on her father.

"We can't do this here." Rick manhandled Jack into the car. So far, no one else had noticed the scuffle, but he couldn't count on that for much longer.

"How long have you known?" she repeated louder. All the warmth and trust they'd been building these last few days evaporated.

Rick took the phone from her. His fingertips brushed against her cold hand. "Pete, we're on our way back... yeah, I've got him."

Jessie remained rooted to the spot, disbelief carved onto her beautiful face. They had to get out of there before someone else saw Jack. "You coming?" he asked.

She got into the car.

Beth moved like she and Steadman were going to follow, but Rick blocked them. "Just her."

Beth's eyes darkened. Mamma bears did not like being separated from their cubs.

Her dad was back. Here. In Chenaniah River. Rick knew. He didn't tell her. Her mind couldn't process anything beyond those basic thoughts.

Rick drove without speaking, clenching and unclenching the steering wheel. A muscle in his jaw repeatedly twitched as the only indicator that her dad's attack had rattled him.

She connected her father's blue jacket to the man from the surveillance video and the one who disrupted the funeral. It wasn't hard to connect the dots from there. Dad had been here a while and didn't bother to see her. She wasn't sure which wound hurt more, her dad's fresh betrayal or Rick's silence regarding his presence. "How long have you known?" she repeated. She'd ask however many times it took to get an answer.

Rick's gaze flicked her way. "That your dad was back? Since the funeral."

"How long have you known he was the one who left the note on my car?" The message that wasn't trying to scare her but protect her. Warn her. Do what a father does.

It rattled her.

"After your allergy attack, I was able to speak with your father. He told us then."

"Us? Who's us?" Her attack was two days ago. For

two days, Rick sat on the most important piece of information. Her wayward father had returned.

"I wanted to tell you, Jessie. They wouldn't let me," Dad piped up from the back.

"That's not entirely true. When I caught you at the funeral, you said she can't know that you're here," Rick said.

Jessie flinched. Her dad came for Frankie, not her. "Who are they?" She forced the words out between clenched teeth.

"Give me five more minutes to get to the safe house, and you'll get some answers."

Safe house? Rick watched his mirrors as they drove in circles, backtracking before moving forward.

"What are you doing? What's taking so long?" Dad complained from the back.

"Making sure that no one is following us. After your stupid actions back there, you might have blown the whole case." Rick eyeballed her dad through the rear-view mirror.

Blown the case? What was Rick talking about? How was her dad involved? How could they converse like any of this was normal?

"Your friend here is an undercover RCMP officer," Dad spat.

Rick winced.

"What?" Her gaze swiveled back to Rick. Had

anything he'd told her since she arrived been the truth?

Rick pulled in front of a cabin tucked into a secluded wooded area. A man waiting on the porch jogged to the car as Rick parked. He yanked open the back door.

"Are you trying to get yourself killed?" The man pulled her father out of the vehicle and hauled him none to gently up the steps and into the house.

"I'm not going to sit by while some psychopath tries to off my daughter." Dad's voice carried back to Jessie.

She scrambled after them, not waiting for Rick. The men continued to argue about the foolishness of Dad's actions.

"I'm not under arrest. You can't force me to stay," Dad said.

"Maybe not." Rick came up behind and darted around Jessie. He levelled such a fierce look at her father that it made Jessie squirm. "But if you want to stay alive long enough to find Frankie's killer, you need us." He stomped up the porch steps and preceded her into the house.

"Someone tell me what is going on!" Jessie slammed the front door so hard it rattled the dishes in the cupboard. All three men looked at her. Finally.

"Hi, I'm Pete Ryerse. We spoke on the phone." The stranger stepped forward and thrust out his hand as if they were meeting over dinner or something.

She ignored his hand.

He dropped it to his side. "Look, I get that you want answers, but right now we can't give you any. This is an active case."

Her gaze spun to Rick, who flinched. Were they shutting her out? "You said I'd get some answers."

"I did, and you will, but evidently not today."

"You've got to be kidding me. Someone has tried to kill me multiple times. I deserve answers."

Rick nodded, but Pete spoke. "It's not Rick's call to make. It's mine."

She spun herself around and faced him head on.

Pete stepped back.

She moved toward him while clenching and unclenching her fists at her side. "I am up to my neck in this. I deserve something."

"I understand you feel that way, but you're not entitled to anything. You have to trust us."

Trust Rick? Pete? Her dad? She squeezed her eyes shut. As far as she was concerned, none of them deserved her trust.

Chapter 14

The haunting disappointment in Jessie's eyes speared right through Rick. The fact that his inaction intensified the blows she was forced to absorb twisted the knife deeper into his gut. Jessie flinched with each syllable Pete spoke.

Now, after an unsatisfying hour of her drilling Pete but receiving no answers, she sat beside him in the front passenger seat, physically close but emotionally distant. Tight lips stretched across her porcelain face. Her nostrils flared with each noisy inhalation. Her chin thrust upward, and flinty eyes dared him to speak. He bit back words. Nothing could fix this except information he wasn't authorized to give.

He pulled the car up to Frankie's place and cut the engine. She wasn't going to take what he had to say well. The back of his throat ached at the necessary words. "It's not safe for you to stay here. We'll gather a few things, and

I'll take you to Steadman's or Aunt Norma's place. You pick."

She shot him an uninviting glare.

"The attacks are getting more and more aggressive. It's quite clear that my staying in the kennels is not enough to protect you."

She lifted a single eyebrow and cocked her head, controlling her words. "I'm not leaving. I'm not done searching the house." She broke eye contact and stared straight ahead, her arms folded across her chest. "But you can bunk on the couch. I'll move into my dad's old room. It has a lock." It was clear that was the only concession she was willing to offer. Rick decided to take the victory.

He nodded his agreement. It wasn't ideal, but it would have to do. "Wait here until I wave you in."

"Fine."

He got out of the car. She hadn't offered more than a basic answer to his direct questions since they left the safe house. The tension between them wasn't going to blow over. Instead, it seemed to be stirring into the storm of the century. Her doubts stiffened his back, but his job wasn't to gain her trust. His job was to keep her alive. If he had to choose between gaining her confidence or saving her life, he'd choose life.

After a quick property check, inside and out, he waved her inside and commanded Max to guard. Too soon, he faced her closed bedroom door. The lock clunked with finality as she slid it into place. Whatever they might have been building between them had dissolved the second she saw her father.

He returned to the kennel to gather a few of his things and care for the animals. He opened the doors to release Frankie's dogs, and the puppies all scrambled through the gate into the fenced yard except two, Duke and Daisy. Two clumsy paws landed on his chest. "Down, Duke."

Duke immediately landed on his hind end. His bottom wiggled, and his tail thumped the floor. Duke's sister, Daisy, nosed her face into Rick's open palm. Her slobbery tongue filled his hand with the best kiss he'd had in months and, if Jessie's coolness was any indication, nothing better was on the horizon.

"Thata girl." He scratched behind her ears. "At least you still love me."

She rewarded him with a yip of playfulness and bounded away.

He filled bowls with dog food and fresh water and left the doors open so the dogs could come and go at their leisure. He returned to the main house. Jessie had stacked some blankets and a pillow on the couch while he was out. He made up his bed, and Max settled on the carpet at his feet. Could he have done anything differently with Jessie? Should he have told her about Jack? If she weren't his friend—if she were just a case—would he second guess himself like this?

He propped his feet up on the coffee table and watched as the accumulating snow buried his footprints from his patrol around the exterior of the house. If only it were that easy to erase the imprint Jessie had made on his heart. Maybe then he'd have the objectivity he needed to do his job well.

He opened his Bible to Proverbs and started where he had left off yesterday at the tenth verse of chapter nine. He clicked a pen and underlined: *The fear of the Lord is the beginning of wisdom.* He jotted in the margin. *It is wise to fear and obey God. How do the half-truths necessary for my work honor the Lord? Can I do this job and be a man of God?*

He prayed until the sun slipped beneath the edge of the earth and the evening cold seeped through the walls. He woke, hours later, with his Bible still open on his lap. He dragged a hand down over his face and arched the kinks out of his back. Max lifted his head and then settled back down.

"Too early for you?" He ruffled the hairs on the dog's head and tapped his phone. 6:30 in the morning. The winter sun still hid behind the curvature of the earth, and shadowy patches of snow dampened the usual morning sounds.

His phone beeped, and Rick jumped.

Everything good? Pete texted.

Good wasn't the word he'd choose.

He texted back. *All's quiet.*

Maybe too quiet. The still wind and utter silence sent a shudder up his back. Max lay undisturbed at his feet. If anything were amiss, Max would know. Rick forced his muscles to relax.

Pete texted again. *Did some digging into Officer Thorn as you suggested. He has bit too much money for a single income family. Can you follow up?*

Will do. He tapped the phone screen, and it went dark.

Rick rubbed his hand over his five o'clock shadow and recalled what he knew about the young officer. Recently married. High maintenance wife. If the overheard phone calls were reliable, their honeymoon ended a long time ago.

A light flicked on in the kitchen. Max lifted his head at the padding of slippered feet. The doorway framed Jessie perfectly. Her hair, all mussed from a night's sleep, fell softly around her face. His pulse throbbed in his throat and his mouth dried up at the unexpected glimpse of her all vulnerable and soft.

Staying here might not have been his wisest decision. There was something strangely intimate about Jessie with sleep in her eyes and flashes of her nightshirt peeking through her tattered robe.

She plunked a mug on the countertop, reached for the

coffee tin and stuffed in a measuring spoon to scoop out the ground coffee. She shook the tin, and then slammed it down on the counter. She tossed the spoon into the sink and returned the mug to its shelf.

He clucked his tongue. This was not the day for her to run out of coffee.

He cleared his throat and stood. "I need to get something from the kennel. I'll be right back."

She briefly clenched her hands before nodding. She never even looked at him.

About fifteen minutes later he found her in the living room petting Max. He held out a caffeinated peace offering. "It's just the way you like it."

Her mouth gaped open, and she eyed him with suspicion, but she accepted the cup. The dark under her eyes proved her night hadn't been any better than his, but she looked adorable, nonetheless.

He had a sudden urge to drop his head and kiss away the dumbfounded expression on her face. He postured against it. She'd made her feelings pretty clear. "I thought, since it was early, you might need a cup. Two creams, two sugars. That's right, isn't it?"

"Yes," she whispered.

"Don't look so shocked. I'm a pretty nice guy." He nudged her shoulder.

She stiffened at his touch. "It's just, ahh, I don't often

get what I want."

He winced. If he could go back in time and give Jessie what she wanted, he would. He'd save her brother... talk some sense into her negligent father... might even try to get Pete to tell her more about her dad. But he couldn't. All he could do was give her right now. He could give her as much honesty as his job allowed. He could respect the new boundaries she had drawn around their friendship.

He rocked back onto his heels shifting his frame out of the hot zone that vibrated between them. But instead of dissolving the zinging heat, it stirred it even more. "What are your plans for today?"

The corner of her lips lifted, but the small smile didn't quite reach her dark-rimmed eyes. "A little sleuthing."

Coldness hit his core. "Tell me you're kidding."

"Oh, don't get that scrunchy face." She stood up and brushed past Rick, retreating into the kitchen. She placed her coffee on the table.

He followed. She was not getting off the hook that easily.

"I'm not leaving the house." She pulled some papers out of her satchel. "Frankie had been looking into the closure of Eastmore. He had downloaded a bunch of newspaper articles about other factories closing in similar circumstances and printed them out. It seems like he believed the company defaulted on the pensions legally.

Something about the government allowing underfunded pensions." She held out the papers to him.

This lined up with the research Daniel had found on Frankie's computer. "Why would Frankie be looking into the pension money?"

She shrugged. "Maybe Frankie was trying to clear Dad's name?"

"If the factory forfeited on the pensions legally, then your dad didn't steal the money." He looked up from the papers. "He was framed."

"It's beginning to look like it." She folded her arms across her chest in a protective way. Was she trying to protect herself from him or from the idea that her dad had been innocent all along, and she never believed him?

He gently squeezed her upper arm. "This is a huge break."

She shook her head. "If Dad was uninvolved and I didn't believe him…" She tightened one arm around her middle and played with the pendant at her neck. She pulled her bottom lip into her mouth and bit down. The silence stretched out.

"That's a pretty necklace," Rick said it more to fill the awkward moment than anything else. There was nothing he could do to rewrite her history with her father. Nothing he could say to make her earlier harsh assumptions any less wrong.

She pulled out the charm far enough that she could see it. "It was my mother's." She released it, and it landed just below her throat at the collarbone.

"I've always admired it. I've never seen anything like it." He gently lifted it from her neck. His fingers grazed her collarbone, and goosebumps freckled her skin.

She turned her face away as her cheeks turned pink. She tightened the belt on her robe.

Warmth flooded him, and he fought a smile. She could deny it all she wanted, but a body didn't lie. She might be angry with him, but she wasn't indifferent. Not in the slightest.

His voice deepened, "Are those river pebbles?" He turned the pendant over in his fingers. Five small stacked stones.

"Yes." She cleared her throat and stepped back from him. The pendant slipped from his fingers and thumped against her collarbone. She picked up her drink like a shield. "It's a pile of stones, like the Israelites built in the Old Testament."

"I'm familiar with the story. It's a tribute to answered prayers." A pile of stones was a reminder of God's provision, meant to help a person set aside anxiety about the future.

"Except all my life my prayers have brought me more confusion than peace."

Her Bible sat opened on the table with a pen resting in the seam. At least she was looking for answers in the right place. "Maybe you're praying with the wrong expectations."

She wrinkled her brow. "What's that supposed to mean?"

"When Sarah called me the night she died, I prayed for wisdom and discernment. I *expected* things would be fine."

"But she died."

"It shook me. I had been asking God to increase my faith, and instead of giving me easy answers, He put me into situations that proved I couldn't rely on myself. I needed Him."

"So, her death was God's answer to your prayer?"

"No, that's not what I mean." Rick rubbed a hand over his face. How could he communicate what was in his heart without misrepresenting God? "I kept asking God to be near me, but I forgot the passages of Scripture that tell me He is near the broken-hearted. Sometimes the things we see as problems are really God's answer to our prayers." The Lord had been teaching him so much these past few years of undercover work.

She arched a perfectly shaped brow and huffed. "That's not a ringing endorsement for prayer."

"That's a bit short-sighted. Jesus tells us to ask so our joy can be made full. The road to joy might be harder, but in the end, God's not ever gonna let you down."

Her eyes shuttered, and she subtly turned away under the guise of fiddling with her coffee cup. "God isn't the one who let me down," she murmured.

Granted, he didn't tell her about her dad, but she had to understand that his job required him to be evasive. Surely, she knew that he was on her side? He reached out for her hand, but she pulled it out of reach. His gesture fell flat. He hooked his thumbs through his belt loops.

She wrapped her arms around her body. She was the kind of person who'd drive back to the bank to return a pen she accidentally pocketed. She would never see the necessary evils of his job the way he saw them. Her life was black and white, and his job forced him to live in the gray.

"Come on, Jessie. Don't lose hope now."

She squeezed her eyes shut. "It hurts too much to hope."

He forced a tight smile. That's right. He had let Jessie down. "I'll go check on the dogs."

She placed a hand on his arm and stopped him from leaving. "Can we go to the cemetery today?"

Maybe it was the way she slightly tightened her fingers. Maybe it was the way her eyes softened or how she waited for his response with an expression of hopefulness mixed with dread. Whatever the reason, he quickly agreed.

"We'll have to drive separately. I need to stop at the station afterward."

"Thanks. Just give me a few minutes." She scurried upstairs.

What was he thinking? He was here to solve a case, not date the girl. Unfortunately, it was becoming clear that she wasn't just any ordinary girl.

Chapter 15

Jessie powered through her morning routine. She didn't want to keep Rick waiting. Then, she didn't want to think about why she didn't want to keep him waiting. There was this strange push and pull with Rick that left her unsettled. She wanted to believe he had her best interests at heart, but if he did, why did he lie to her? Why didn't he tell her about her dad? If he was capable of keeping that a secret, what else was he keeping from her?

She snagged her loner phone from the bedside table and paused. She activated the recorder app and dictated a note. *Is Rick trustworthy? Where was he when I was pushed on the ice? Did he stage accidents that would force me to trust him? He's saved me over and over. Am I that lucky, or is Rick involved? What about what the reporter said?*

She pressed save and ignored the feelings of betrayal that stirred as she spoke her doubts out loud. In her heart, she believed him, but her writer mind had a way of processing things, and she needed to respect the process if she ever hoped to make sense of this muddled mess. Frankie had always said she'd make a great reporter.

Her stomach somersaulted. She hadn't even had time yet to grieve Frankie. He had been more than her brother. He was her friend and her biggest encourager. When Frankie confided his mistrust of the local police, she had assumed he meant everyone except Rick, but maybe not? She took Rick at his word that Frankie had invited him into the case. But Rick was, after all, on the police force. Don't those guys stick together? If only Frankie were still here. He'd help her sort it out.

Within thirty minutes Jessie was sitting on the bench she had placed on Frankie's grave, and Rick stood off to the side like some secret service agent on protective duty.

The idea of a tombstone had seemed too final. She wanted something that invited her to linger. She had engraved the Bible verse that changed Frankie's life onto the seat, Titus 3:5-6. *He saved us, not because of works done by us in righteousness, but according to his own mercy, by the washing of regeneration and renewal of the Holy Spirit, whom he poured out on us richly through Jesus Christ our Savior.*

She'd buried Frankie beside her mom, who also believed in salvation through faith in Jesus. A tear tracked down her cheek.

Rick respectfully diverted his eyes.

She believed that too, but it was easier before all this loss. *God, are You still there? I know your Word says that You'll never leave me, but I feel alone down here. I could use a friend.*

Rick coughed.

She hid a smile. *That wasn't the friend I had in mind, Lord.*

Rick didn't look at her. He stared toward the mound of earth covered in snow, still slightly higher than the surrounding graves. Frankie hadn't been buried long enough for the ground to settle.

She wiped her face. "You're probably ready to go."

"You can take all the time you need." He kept his eyes averted as if he was trying to offer her privacy.

She studied his profile but veered her eyes when he caught her. She couldn't figure Rick out. He was a paradox. A bargain-priced hero. He was noble and honorable on the one hand, and secretive and less than perfect on the other. Which face was the real man?

They stayed like that for some time. Comfortable. Quiet. Still. Eventually, she asked the question pressing on her heart. "If God is so good, why didn't He create a good world?"

Rick shoved his hands into his pockets and hunkered

down into his heavy jacket. His rosy cheeks and snow-covered hair told her that he must be uncomfortable, yet he had stayed without complaint of the worsening weather conditions. "God did make a good world. In fact, it was perfect, but we no longer live in that world."

"And we have to deal with suffering, addiction, and death. It's not fair." She didn't know why she felt like blaming him. Her expectations were unrealistic. It wasn't like he could fix anything or change anything.

He pointed to the bench. "May I?"

She scooted over. Rick wiped off the snow that had accumulated and sat beside her. He shifted toward Jessie, and their knees touched. "The world's brokenness is part of the punishment for the sin that ruined God's perfect world."

"But why?" She lifted her face to the biting wind. Somehow the cold against her cheeks soothed the burning in her heart. "Why would God let it be like this for so long?"

He shrugged. "I don't know for sure, but maybe to give us a taste of what life is like without Him."

There were no easy answers. Jessie knew that. Snow swirled across the cemetery in a growing dust devil fashion. A storm was blowing in fast. "We should go." She glanced back to where she had parked her car. Rick had pulled his vehicle beside it. She squinted. "Is someone in my car?" For a brief second, the interior light flickered brightly against the darkened and stormy sky before falling dark again.

Rick leaped to his feet and sprinted to the vehicles.

There were only three cars in the parking lot: hers, Rick's, and a town truck. She hadn't noticed the town vehicle when she arrived. The workers were all over Chenaniah River keeping things in good repair for the festival.

Rick reached the front bumper of his car. In two more steps, he'd be right on top of the intruder.

She held her breath. *Could this be it, Lord? Will it all end here and now?*

She lagged a few steps behind Rick and strained to listen. Was that movement? The hum of traffic as folks made their morning commute? The falling snow messing with her mind? Her hands sweated inside her gloves.

Rick circled both vehicles. "No one's here."

She followed him back to her car. There were no marks, no scratches, nothing. "I know I saw the interior light. And the snow is disturbed along the top of the door."

Rick pressed his lips together. He looked underneath the edges of the trunk and ran his fingers underneath the lip. He walked around to the front of the car and repeated the actions at the hood.

She reached out to try the handle.

"Don't!"

Her arm froze in mid-air at his sharp command. "I was checking it see if it's unlocked."

"Don't touch anything until I'm finished." He dropped to his hands and knees and used the flashlight app on his phone to search underneath the carriage of the car.

Was he looking for a bomb? She gently rested her hand on the car top to steady her shaky legs then jerked it back. *Hands off.*

He wriggled himself under the vehicle. The wet from the snow had to be seeping through his jacket by now. The flashlight beam spilled out from underneath. Finally, he pulled himself out and stood. "Looks good." He put his hand on the driver's side door handle and paused. "But maybe you should stand back, you know, just in case."

Jessie scrambled back a few steps. Her heart beat in her throat.

Rick tugged on the handle. The interior lit up as the dome light clicked on. He met her gaze. "Could you have left it unlocked?"

"I know I locked it, especially considering everything that has happened."

Rick crouched down, still outside the vehicle, and looked under the driver's seat and all around the pedals. He walked to the passenger side and repeated the search. Then he popped the trunk. "Anything amiss?"

She looked in. "Nope."

He lifted the hood and studied the engine.

She looked over his shoulder. "What are you looking for?"

"Extra switches or wires. Anything that doesn't belong."

A cold zipped down her back that had nothing to do with the impending storm.

"Look through the glove compartment and see if anything is missing while I check the wheel wells."

She rifled through the glove compartment and then expanded her search into every compartment but found nothing out of place. Could she have imagined it? "Maybe it was just a reflection like you said," she called out.

"No, it wasn't." He stood outside her open door and held out a small device about the size of a cell phone. He'd already encased it in a plastic bag. "It's a GPS tracker."

"Someone's been following me?" Her fingers spread across her neck as a feeling of violation swept over her.

"Or someone planned to follow you." He helped her out of her car and locked the doors before closing them. "You're not going anywhere in that vehicle until we give it a good once over. I want the brakes and all the mechanical stuff checked out. If they left this, who knows what other surprises they've planned. And if they were inside, they may have planted a microphone."

She scanned the area. Nothing but tombstones faintly visible in the blinding snow surrounded them. Was someone watching them now? Was someone waiting for the chance to strike? She stepped closer to Rick. "What do we do now?"

He opened his passenger side door and gestured to the front seat. "Consider me your chauffeur."

She climbed in. Her head was swimming with questions.

"I'll drive you home, get a team here to check out your vehicle, and drop this..." He wiggled the GPS device. "...off at the station." Rick pulled his vehicle onto the road behind a painfully slow-moving black Taurus with a blue-haired grandma behind the wheel. "I'll retrieve your phone then as well. You can have it back now that Daniel is finished with it."

The falling snowflakes fattened with each passing second and swirled like the questions in her mind. Who had targeted her? Why? Did someone really sabotage her car?

Rick flipped the wipers on high and put the radio on the local weather station. The weatherman's deep baritone gave a warning. *Chenaniah River is under a winter storm warning. A significant combination of hazardous winter weather is occurring or imminent. We expect to see five inches or more of snow and sleet within the next twelve-hour period and enough ice accumulation to cause damage to trees or power lines. This could be a life-threatening combination of wind, snow and ice. Take care out there. If you don't need to be on the road, stay indoors.*

"Come on, Grandma." Jessie tapped her foot on the floor.

The passing lane cleared, and Rick pulled out and hit the gas. The blowing snow blurred the yellow center lines on the road.

Rick merged back in his lane and turned off the main road. Grandma had followed their turn again. Jessie stretched her tingling neck trying to will herself to relax. She forced her shoulders down and tipped her head to the side, elongating the tight muscles. It wasn't like some old lady was going to jump out of a moving vehicle wielding a weapon of mass destruction. She flicked her eyes to Grandma again and giggled at the idea of some curly gray-haired ninja.

Out of nowhere a white pickup zipped from behind and slipped in between them and the lagging grandma. It had an orange stripe across the door, like the logo of Chenaniah River Public Works vehicles. Like the one at the cemetery.

"Rick—"

"I see it." His gaze alternated from the truck in the rear-view mirror to the snow squall building in front of them. He flexed his fingers on the steering wheel. "Can you make out the license plate?"

She cranked her neck around. "The truck is too close."

Rick let off on the gas. "Maybe he'll pass us."

The truck slowed to match their speed. "He's got a ski mask on." Her stomach knotted. "That's not good, is it?"

"Doesn't feel good." A muscle in Rick's jaw twitched. The truck crept so close that if Rick even tapped the brakes their stalker would be in their back seat.

Rick sped up. The driver made a gun with his index and thumb and pointed it at them. She gasped. Did Rick see that?

"Call the police station." Rick held out his phone. "Speed dial two."

She fumbled with it and punched the programmed number.

"Hold on!" Rick cranked the wheel and the car careened around a corner without slowing down.

"Chenaniah Police."

"This is Jessie Berns. I'm with Detective Rick Chandler. Someone's following us. I think they're trying to run us off the road." She grabbed the dash with one hand as Rick jerked the wheel again.

"Where are you?"

Rick took another hard turn, hit the gravel shoulder, and overcorrected. The phone flew from her hand and tumbled across her feet, landing under the seat just out of reach.

"Hello? Hello?" The faint voice of the operator rose from where the phone had wedged itself.

Rick floored it. "We're on Valley Road headed north," he shouted. "We just left the cemetery."

The truck behind them roared and bumped their back end. Metal crunched metal. The car swayed. Rick yanked the wheel to the left, and their back end slid across the entire lane spinning them sideways. He overcorrected again, pulling to the right.

A faint silhouette of oncoming traffic emerged from the swirling snow.

"No, no, no!" He cranked the wheel toward the ditch. "Hold on!"

Jessie braced for impact.

"Are you okay?" Rick asked. The car rested at an angle, the front end tunneled into a snow bank and wedged into the ditch. A hiss of air filled the inside of the vehicle as the airbags deflated.

"I'm okay."

Outside of losing a bit of color in her cheeks, Jessie appeared unscathed. Rick's heart thudded against his ribs. *Thank you, Lord, for soft snow!*

Jessie rotated her neck and shoulders. "I'm fine," she repeated.

"Is everyone okay?" The operator's voice sounded from under the seat. Rick slit his seat belt with a knife he kept clipped to the visor and freed himself. He ran his hands down Jessie's neck, shoulders, and arms. He looked into her eyes. "I'm gonna get that phone, and then I'll cut you loose." He felt around under the seat.

"He's stopping!" Jessie's panic filled the car. She pulled on her seatbelt.

At the top of the ditch, the man climbed out of his truck. Rick strained to reach the phone.

"I can't get out! My seatbelt's stuck!" She yanked on the clasp.

Rick's fingers wrapped around the phone. He pulled it out from under the seat. "This is Officer Rick Chandler. I have a 10-31 on Valley Road. Officer in need of back-up."

"10-4."

He sliced Jessie's seat belt with the knife and freed her. "We need to get out of the car." He looked along the ditch. They might be able to find cover in the reeds, but they wouldn't last long in the worsening elements.

She nodded.

Rick tracked the man watching them from the top of the ditch. Two more vehicles stopped.

"It's the grandma!" Jessie pointed at the elderly

woman they passed earlier as Rick eased her out the door.

"Stay low." He forced her head down in case their friend brought his rifle.

"There's someone else, too." Rick peeked over the trunk and squinted at a young man who leaped from his sedan started down the ditch toward the car. Friend or foe?

"Are you okay?" he called as he descended.

The truck driver's head swiveled from them to the Good Samaritan. He climbed back into his vehicle and left.

Rick sagged, partly in relief and partly in frustration. How many more times would they get this close to their pursuer and lose him?

"Are you okay?' the man huffed.

"Yes." Rick flashed his badge. "Did you happen to get the license of that truck?"

"No, I didn't think to look." Their Samaritan looked up at the spot where the truck had idled just a few minutes before. It was hard to see anything in the growing blizzard, but from what Rick could tell, Grandma had moved on as well.

Within a few minutes, Gavin and the chief arrived. Rick helped Jessie into the back of a warm vehicle and wrapped her in a blanket. He debriefed the chief about the vehicle tampering at the cemetery right up to when Rick ditched the car. "The truck looked like our town vehicles. It had an orange horizontal stripe across the door."

"If they're after her and her car is still at the cemetery, why did they follow you?"

Rick pulled out the GPS out of his pocket. "Because I had this. It was stuck in the wheel well of her car." The idea that someone had planned to follow Jessie and run her off the road soured Rick's stomach. What would have happened if he hadn't been there?

The chief pulled out a proper evidence bag and held it open for Rick to drop the GPS inside.

Rick flicked his gaze to Jessie still bundled in the vehicle and watching them intently. Jessie unrolled the car window. "The guy bumped us on the back end," he said. "Not too hard but hard enough to leave a mark. It forced me into the curve too fast, and I lost control. If we find a town truck with damage from a minor collision, we'll have our guy."

"Tell me about the man who stopped." The chief frowned at Jessie, who still watched Rick with a combination of gratitude and awe etched on her face.

Rick's heart did a funny flop. There was no way she was just Frankie's sister. Somewhere along the line, she had become so much more.

Brewer's scowl deepened.

"He had on a ski mask," Jessie said. "I couldn't see much of him. I'm sorry I can't be more helpful. Hopefully, Rick has more details."

Brewer gave Rick a meaningful look. Rick cleared his throat. "By the time we got out of the car he was gone. Even the tire tracks had filled with snow."

"He took off when other vehicles slowed down to see if we were okay," Jessie filled in.

"Thank you, Ms. Berns." Brewer led Rick a few steps away. "I think you should take her to the hospital. Headaches, mental fogginess, and anxiety are all part of a post-concussive syndrome."

"But her speech isn't slurred, and she's not overly irritable. She's fine." No way was he bringing her to the hospital. If word got out that she was there, she'd be an easy target.

Brewer flipped the bagged GPS over in his hand. "Don't you find it interesting that every time we turn around this woman is in danger? Could she be trumping up the danger to snag herself attention or..." He paused. "...to snag herself a man?"

A small gasp came from the car. Rick's stomach heaved. Was Jessie's window still open?

"I'm beginning to see a pattern here, Rick. We don't need another woman vying for your attention."

He gritted his teeth. "I understand, sir, but she did not imagine this. I was there."

"Get her out of here." Brewer pressed a set of keys into Rick's hands. "We'll talk later."

Rick turned back to the car, where Jessie appeared to be on the phone. Gavin stood off to the side surveying the area. She disconnected as Rick approached and handed the phone back to Gavin through her open window. "Thanks." She looked at Rick. "Mine is dead."

"Everything okay?"

"I called Steadman and arranged to go over there. I might stay there for a few days. I don't know."

"That's probably a good idea." For more reasons than she knew. He didn't know if he could take another morning of seeing her in her robe. It was too intimate. Too close. And it stirred a desire for things that his job wouldn't let him have.

He got into the driver's seat. Her expression gave no clue as to how she felt about the chief's comments. She didn't refer to it, so he never brought it up. Maybe she didn't hear. "Do you need to go home first?"

"No, just take me right there."

"The chief gave me this." Rick handed Jessie her old phone as he pulled the vehicle onto the road.

She flipped it over in her hands. "Did Daniel find anything on it?"

"Nothing useful to the case but he was able to recover your contacts and stuff." She dipped her head, and a sheet of dark hair hid her face. She scrolled through her apps.

Was her silence a result of her distraction or because

she had heard the chief? He turned on Bluetooth and tugged his phone from his pocket so it would connect to his playlist. Anything to fill the silence.

"Oh, wait." She rummaged around in her purse and removed the loaner phone he had given her. "Let me give you this before I forget. I think the cold drained the battery."

"Connect it to the in-vehicle charger."

She plugged the phone into the charger, and it beeped loud. Once the loaner charged enough to turn on, it automatically connected to the Bluetooth system and Jessie's voice came over the sound system.

Is Rick trustworthy? Where was he when I was pushed on the ice? Did he stage accidents that would force me to trust him? He's saved me over and over. Am I really that lucky, or is Rick involved? What about what the reporter said?

"What's happening? Turn it off!" She slapped at buttons on the dash. "Turn it off!" Unable to find the disconnect button, she twisted the volume knob. Silence descended.

Rick stared at Jessie's profile. "You think I'm involved? Do you think I killed Frankie too?"

Chapter 16

Jessie's insides warmed at the way Beth jumped up from her chair on her covered front porch when Rick pulled the vehicle into the driveway. At least someone was happy to see her.

The second the car stopped, Jessie scrambled from it. She couldn't get out fast enough. A choking silence had followed that dumb recording, and it gave her too much time to think. She didn't want to think about how much it hurt to overhear Rick and the chief question her character. She didn't want to think, didn't want to feel. And she did not want to talk about it.

"Jessie, wait," Rick called her back through his open car window before she could reach the sanctuary of the porch.

She turned.

"You forgot your old phone. I had Daniel install a Find

Your Family app. I accepted the tracking request for you. Please don't uninstall it. It will let me track you if it ever comes to that."

Rick extended his arm out the window to hand her the phone. His smile didn't quite meet his eyes, and that was her fault too. But she couldn't apologize. What she said about Rick wasn't any worse than what the chief implied about her.

She reluctantly approached the driver's side window, but just as she reached for the phone, he pulled it back.

"I know you're not pleased with me," he said softly enough that Beth couldn't hear from where she waited on the porch tapping her foot impatiently. "By the sound of that recording, you don't even like me. But until we figure out what is going on, you shouldn't be alone. Either call me or stay here. And if you get into trouble, this app will help me find you."

She snagged the phone and nodded her concession. She didn't know which one of them was more shocked by her agreement.

Rick was right. She wasn't too pleased with him. But at the moment, she wasn't too pleased with herself, either. Somehow, despite her resolve to keep her distance from him, he had wormed his way into her heart. It made everything that transpired between them sting more intensely because she could no longer deny that he affected her. The way he made her coffee, remembering how she liked it, the way he instinctively pulled her close when danger loomed, it made her feel protected. Loved.

She swallowed a lump in her throat and shoved the thought away. He didn't love her. This was his job. She suddenly had a deeper appreciation for how easy it must have been for Sarah to fall for Rick. A bond forms when a man risks his life for you, a bond easily mistaken for love and intimacy.

Rick sat in the driveway with the engine idling, waiting for her to enter the house. Even now, he was a gentleman ensuring she was safe before leaving.

Beth called down from the porch. "Would you like to join us, Rick? I always make extra on Sunday."

Jessie froze. She felt Rick's eyes boring into her back.

"That'd be real nice. Thank you."

A foreign feeling rushed over Jessie. She wasn't sure if she was happy or angry that he accepted the invitation. Rick cut the engine and his car door slammed shut. The porch boards creaked under his weight.

Why would he agree? He had to feel the tension between them. He had to know how uncomfortable this made her.

"Jessie, I'm so glad you called." Steadman met her in the foyer and gave her a quick embrace. "Beth's got lunch ready. We figured you hadn't eaten with everything that happened." Steadman's eyes flicked behind her, and they momentarily darkened when they landed on Rick.

"Mr. Mayor." Rick extended his hand. "Your wife kindly invited me to join you."

Steadman shook his hand. "We appreciate all that you've done for Jessie since her return."

Some of the tension eased from Jessie's neck and shoulders as they followed Steadman into the dining room and took their places at the table. Maybe having Steadman as a buffer between her and Rick would smooth things over?

This was the first time she had been in Steadman's house since her family had moved away from Chenaniah River. If décor was any indicator, Steadman had done well for himself after the factory closed. Long curtains billowed on either side of a window covered in a leaded design, and an abundance of antiques filled the space. Each one looked like it had its own story to tell. Expensive looking art covered the walls, but only one picture caught her eye. She stepped closer to examine it. "Where is this?"

"That's one of Frankie's," Steadman said. "It's the old train bridge crossing Chenaniah River."

"It's beautiful." Frankie had captured the silhouette of a lone canoe paddling under the bridge over calm waters.

"He had quite an eye. I'm excited to see how people respond to the art show this year." Steadman rested a hand on her shoulder.

Jessie reached up and covered his hand with her own. "Me too." Above the piano hung a painting of an apple tree in front of an older, more pristine version of her childhood home. "Where did you get this?"

Steadman smiled. "I found it in your attic. Daisy painted it."

"You have keys to the Berns's house?" Rick asked.

"Who is Daisy?" asked Jessie.

Beth swept into the room. "Lunch is ready." She directed them to the table. "Steadman has been taking care of the property since Jessie's dad left. Jack never put it up for sale, so it sat empty until Frankie returned."

"I hope you don't mind." Steadman's brows pulled together with a look of concern.

"Of course, it's fine," Jessie assured him. "It's better that it didn't sit empty."

"According to my research, Daisy is Grandma Maggie's daughter. She dabbled in watercolors. This is rumored to be one of her paintings. Not valuable financially, but irreplaceable to us," Steadman said.

"How did you determine she was the artist?" Rick asked.

"Her initials are in the bottom corner, but Beth found the most convincing evidence. I brought home a stack of diaries, and she has been reading through them."

"Diaries? I didn't know there were diaries."

Steadman unfolded a napkin and laid it across his lap. "Beth found the first one years ago in the attic of our house. She found it long before you ever moved away. It implied there were more, and she's been looking for them ever since. The last time I was at your place before Frankie returned, I found four or five. I brought them home to her."

"Each daughter kept a diary with meticulous notes on family matters," Beth added. "I think we've found them all."

"Isn't the factory built on the same land Daisy painted in the watercolor? It looks like it's by Jessie's place," Rick said.

Beth placed bowls of hot chili in front of them and a loaf of homemade bread in the center of the table.

"Yes. There was controversy when Eastmore built on that land in 1940. The historical society claimed our ancestors..." He included Jessie in the word 'our', "...owned the property on which Eastmore wanted to build. Protestors latched onto that historical connection, citing the legend of the lost diamond as a heritage to protect. The court awarded them four months to search for the missing stone, but it never turned up."

"Enough about that. What happened this morning?" Beth scooped up a spoonful of chili and settled her attention on Jessie.

"It's an open investigation. We can't discuss the details at this point," Rick answered for her.

Beth's concerned expression hardened as she glared at him.

"Surely you can tell us if you have any leads, or if this person targeting Jessie is still a threat?" Steadman fixed such a fearsome stare at Rick that Jessie's stomach quivered.

Rick stared right back without flinching. "The driver might have been in a town vehicle. Any idea who would have access to those?"

Steadman sat back in his chair and stroked his clean-shaven chin. "That could be a number of people. We only have a few trucks, so the keys hang in City Hall and are managed by the administration. I could look into it and see if anyone had it checked out for today."

Rick just stared.

"He's trying to help," Jessie said.

"I'll follow-up myself, but thanks. The information is helpful."

"Have you heard any more from your dad?" Beth asked.

Jessie inhaled the spicy steam wafting upward from her bowl. "The police won't tell me where Dad is, only that he is in protective custody."

Steadman's gaze darted back to Rick.

Jessie chuckled to herself. Rick wasn't winning any prizes with Steadman tonight.

"That doesn't seem right," Steadman said. "Were you able to speak with him yesterday?" He passed her the butter.

"Yeah, but they moved him again after I left. It seems they are not sure who to trust." She kept her eyes on her lunch. Rick remained suspiciously quiet. It was his fault if he was uncomfortable. He accepted the invitation to lunch. She had no reason to feel guilty for answering their questions honestly. But if that were true, why did she?

Beth clucked her tongue. "Seems to me they could trust his daughter."

Beth's correction was intended for Rick, but her words hit Jessie hard. Dad should have been able to count on her. But she, along with the rest of the town, had believed the worst about him. Shame filled Jessie's heart. Steadman and Beth still believed Dad stole the money.

Like he could read her mind, Rick shook his head no.

"Are you okay, Jessie? You look flushed." Steadman and Beth had laid their utensils down and were looking at her with concern.

"No, I'm not okay," her voice cracked. She took a deep breath.

"Jessie, I don't think—"

"Dad didn't steal the pension money," she blurted.

"The factory defaulted legally."

Rick's eyes darkened.

"They deserve to know," she said softly.

Beth's cheeks flamed. "How long did you plan to keep this from us?" she asked Rick.

"As long as I needed to." Rick didn't apologize.

"That's ridiculous," Beth scoffed. "If Jessie uncovered it, it's hardly top secret." She turned to her husband. "Didn't you try to clear his name?"

"Yes, I did." Steadman dabbed the corners of his mouth with his napkin. "I never found anything to prove Jack took the money, but I also found nothing to exonerate him. What sort of proof do you have?"

Jessie ignored Rick's glare. "There were some papers Frankie left in the spare room. He was researching the plant closure and other similar closings. I was going through them." She wiped her nose with her napkin. "What if Dad is innocent and I blamed him all this time? How will he ever forgive me?"

The phone rang. Beth checked the caller ID. "Excuse me. I have to take this. It's work." She hurried out of the room.

"I assumed, with you being mayor and all, that she had stopped working." Rick followed Beth with his eyes.

"She doesn't consult often, only once in a while. Sometimes, former clients will call on her corporate law expertise. Mostly her hours are filled with volunteer work for the Winter Diamond Festival."

"How did you get that started?" Rick had smoothly redirected the topic of conversation away from Jessie's dad.

Steadman's face lit up with a look of pride. "We took the slowest month in the business year, February, and created a marketing campaign that really paid off. When you combine a lost diamond with Valentine's Day, throw in a black-tie event and fun family activities, you end up with a town everyone wants to visit."

But not one where everyone was welcome, Jessie thought.

The next day Rick sat in the chief's office flipping through pictures, but his mind strayed to Jessie. His heart lurched as Jessie's recorded doubts about him replayed in his head. She thought he might have pushed her that night at the river. At best he was suspect, at worst a murderer. Over and over like a repeating song, her doubts echoed that hack reporter's refrain—is Rick trustworthy? Is Rick honorable? Is Rick good at his job?

"Rick?" Brewer jabbed him. "You listening?"

"Yeah." Rick shifted his weight from his left foot to

his right and plucked a random picture off the chief's desktop. "So, this happened in the city? On my old beat?"

"The sorority house is trashed. These are the social media pictures readily available online. Your former captain wants to know if any of these faces are on our radar here, or if you recognize anyone from your work there." Brewer's eyes drilled into his profile.

He'd done some undercover work at the university, but nothing ever came of it.

"If you have something more important to do…" Brewer's voice trailed off but left no misconception that nothing but Rick's full attention was acceptable.

"Nope, I'm good." Rick picked up another picture, and then another. He studied the scenes of intoxicated students dancing, hooking up, and getting high. It was familiar and sad. Some of the brightest minds of the future were too stupid to understand the gamble of drugs, sex, and alcohol.

He flipped through the images at a steady pace. Nope. Nope. Nope. Wait—he looked closer. "Who's this guy?" He pointed to a lanky man with shaggy hair. The camera caught him head on, eyes locked with the camera. Another picture showed him getting out of a gray compact car.

Brewer rifled through some pages in a file folder. "They have noted him as someone to watch for drug trafficking. They haven't been able to nail him yet."

"Or they are letting him sell, waiting for him to lead

them to a bigger fish.''

''Do you know him?''

''I can't place him, but something about his face is familiar.''

''Maybe from when you worked in the city?''

''Maybe.'' But it felt like something more. ''Chenaniah Manor!'' He snapped his fingers. ''I saw him there the day Jessie was attacked, getting off the elevator. He drives the same kind of car that Jessie keeps seeing.''

''Then it's time to head back to Chenaniah Manor and rattle some cages.''

''Yes, sir.''

''Report back to me afterward.''

In less than fifteen minutes, Rick was people-watching in the lobby of Chenaniah Manor. Derek answered the phone and juggled requests from residents. The elevator dinged, and Mr. Broadwick limped out.

He hobbled over to the service desk, painfully favoring one knee and wincing with each step. He white-knuckled the cane for support as Jessie scooted along on his left, helping him by holding his arm.

What was she doing here?

He stormed over. ''I thought I told you not to go anywhere alone?''

''I'm not alone,'' she bristled, steering the old man to the front desk. ''Steadman dropped me off. He'll be back in a few minutes."

She turned toward Derek. "Mr. Broadwick is still in too much pain for post surgery. I think he needs to have his meds reviewed."

"I told her not to bother you," Mr. Broadwick apologized, "but she wouldn't let it go."

"It's no problem, Mr. Broadwick," Derek assured him. "We'll look into it. We don't want you to be uncomfortable."

"See," Jessie beamed at the grandfatherly man. "I told you Derek would look after it. Can you make it the rest of the way to your room?"

"Can do."

As Jessie turned away, Derek exchanged an interesting look with Mr. Broadwick before the old man hobbled back toward the elevator.

Rick calculated the days since the man's surgery. He should be further along by now, and he definitely shouldn't still be in that much pain. "Who is in charge of his medications?" he asked Derek.

"We have a registered nurse that oversees all medical needs. I'll make her aware of this." Derek fidgeted with the pens and papers on his desk.

Rick pulled Jessie aside. "I'm going to slip upstairs to see Mr. Broadwick." He didn't wait for her response. He knew the journalist in her would need to know what he was doing.

They stepped off the elevator just as the old man entered his apartment. Rick rapped on the door. "Your knee still giving you grief?" he asked as soon as it opened.

"Yeah, a bit. Surgery was rough." The man looked past Rick at Jessie.

"Who's in charge of dispensing the pain medication here?"

The briefest micro-expression flickered across Mr. Broadwick's face.

"Ah, they have a nurse for that." Again, he answered as if Jessie had asked, giving her all his attention.

"Does Derek ever manage the pain medication?"

"What are you getting at, Rick?" Jessie stepped out from behind him.

He held up his hand to stop her from interfering. He kept his eyes fixed on Mr. Broadwick.

"No, Derek never manages the pain medication."

Classic deception technique. Answering the question while repeating the question, buys time to think. Rick couldn't prove it was a falsehood, but years of experience told him without a doubt that the man was lying. He looked beyond Mr. Broadwick into the room behind him. A picture of men in camouflage and holding hunting rifles sat on the fireplace mantle. "What's that picture?"

As the old man's eyes followed Rick's gesture, the

door cracked open further, and Rick nudged it open the rest of the way and stepped into the room. Before the man could object, he plucked the framed picture from the mantle.

"That's me and some hunting buddies." Mr. Broadwick seized the picture from Rick and placed it back on the mantle. "And I don't recall inviting you in."

Rick recognized one of the men in the picture as Pat, the resident who had recently lost his wife. He was also around the day the ceramic pot was pushed off the balcony. "Do you still hunt?"

"Not anymore." Stan hobbled the few steps back to the door and motioned it was time for them to leave.

"Come on, Rick." Jessie tugged on his elbow. "Let's go."

Mr. Broadwick slammed the door a little harder than necessary.

A curious neighbor peeked out from his apartment.

"It's okay," Jessie said. "Everything's fine."

As Jessie addressed the neighbor, recognition flashed in the man's eyes. Curiosity turned to anger. It was Pat.

"You're that Berns girl," he spat.

"And I'm Detective Rick Chandler." Rick stepped between them as he flashed his badge. "And you are?"

"Not interested." Pat tried to shut his door, but Rick wedged his foot in it. "It's Pat, right? Recently lost your wife?"

Pat flinched. "What's it to you?"

"Your son was visiting you the other day, wasn't he?"

"Yeah. Rob comes about once a week."

"Were you a part of Stan's hunting club?" He already knew he was from Stan's picture.

"I was. Once."

"Do you have any pictures? Mr. Broadwick just showed us his."

Jessie lifted her eyebrows.

Okay, that was a bit of a stretch. Mr. Broadwick didn't show Rick the pictures as much as Rick had insisted on looking.

"I'll show you, but she can wait out here." The man jutted his chin toward Jessie.

Pictures of Pat and his wife were scattered all over the apartment. Rick tapped one. "Who's this?"

"My son, Rob. He hunts too." Pat handed him a picture of Rob all decked out in hunting gear, holding a Remington .22-250.

"Has your son been hunting lately?"

"He hunts all the time."

"Has he bagged anything lately?" Rick's gaze flicked over several pictures of men posing with their dead game. Not one picture showed Rob with a carcass.

Pat shrugged. "He has a license, and the gun is registered."

Rick swept his gaze over the other photos but didn't hand the one back to Pat. "And what's your problem with Ms. Berns?"

Pat stiffened. "What's that's got to do with anything?"

"Someone used this type of rifle to shoot at her. What were you doing Thursday evening?"

"I was here. Like I always am."

"And your son?"

Pat shrugged.

"Where can I find him?"

"He works for the town."

"Can I hold onto this?" Rick lifted the picture.

Pat nodded.

"Did you find anything helpful?" Jessie whispered as Rick closed the apartment door behind him.

"A lead." Rick phoned Gavin. "I need you to canvass the hunting community. See if anyone can place Pat or Rob Green at either scene where Jessie was shot at."

Jessie looked back at Pat's door.

The old man had cracked it open again and glared at her. He clicked it shut when Rick turned around.

Just what he needed. Jessie making new enemies.

Chapter 17

On Monday morning Jessie stood with her hands on her hips in the center of Frankie's living room. If Frankie had a hidden room like the ones noted in the magazine she'd found at Aunt Norma's, she was going to find it. According to the article she'd left laying open on the kitchen table, carpets often disguised trap doors.

She eyed the large area rug. On it, a couch, occasional chair, coffee table, and two end tables remained in the same places they'd been when she was a young girl. Could a secret room have been under their feet the entire time? Wouldn't her parents have known about it when they moved in? She pushed up the sleeves of her oversized sweatshirt. There was only one way to find out. She shoved the couch back a few feet and grabbed the chair by the sides and dragged it onto the hardwood. She dropped to her knees and started rolling up the carpet.

Max's ears lifted, and he tilted his head as if to ask what she was doing.

"I'm looking for answers, Max." She puffed out a breath, lifting sweaty strands of hair from her face. She dragged the rolled carpet aside.

Max ambled over and laid his head on the rolled-up rug. His dark brown eyes followed her, resigned to a long afternoon.

There were no apparent seams in the flooring, no hinges, or anything that screamed *I'm a door*. She dropped back down to her hands and knees and felt each floorboard one by one. They looked, well, normal. No hidden passageway. Nothing. She repeated the process in every room containing a carpet with no luck. This was going to be harder than she thought.

The article stated the next logical place to search was behind picture frames hanging on the wall. She systematically removed every portrait, painting, and mirror from each wall, hoping to find a safe, or door, or something.

Max followed behind her with a "you're-crazy" look in his eyes.

Maybe she was crazy. She retrieved the magazine from the kitchen. Bookcases were next on the list.

She stretched her sore back, took a swig of water, and headed to the spare bedroom. She groaned at the vast bookshelves lining all four walls. The unneeded room had been turned into a sitting room years ago to give her dad a quiet place to read when she and Frankie were young. He had always been a huge reader, and his personal library was his favorite room in the house.

One by one she removed the books from the shelves and stacked them on the floor in the middle of the room. When she placed the last novel on top of the pile strewn across the floor, she inched the bookcases a few feet from the wall and looked behind.

Max whined.

Nothing. No door. No passageway. Nothing. She was grasping at straws. Even the dog knew it.

Come on, Frankie. Where is it? She ran her hands along the raised-panel trim in the hall as she returned to the kitchen. She pushed on every square inch of wainscoting. She had moved everything not nailed down. She had broken two fingernails and wasted hours.

Hours.

She yanked open the refrigerator and grabbed another bottle of water. She twisted off the top and took a deep drink. The large farmhouse clock ticked noisily, marking the new hour. The ornate clock was original to the house and filled the upper half of one kitchen wall. It had been there as long as she could remember.

She set her bottle on the table and dragged over the

ladder. From the middle rung, she could easily reach the clock. She ran her fingers all around the smooth edges.

Wait, she moved her hand back. A raised lip felt out of place. She precariously leaned over to see behind the edge. Her heart leaped. A hinge! She pulled the clock, but it didn't move. She felt along the backside as far as her fingers could stretch. There! She felt a button, or was it a lever? She pushed it, and a loud click sounded. The clock released as a latch sprung loose. It swung easily away from the wall revealing a small door.

Her blood thundered in her ears. She'd found it! She'd really found it!

Max whined.

"Not now, Max!"

The kitchen doorknob rattled.

She turned slowly from her perch. The knob moved as someone twisted it from the outside. Her throat closed up, and uneasiness filled her gut. She swung the clock back into place, hopped down from the ladder, and grabbed the cast iron frying pan from the stovetop.

She crept toward the door and pressed her back against the wall. She gripped the pan's handle like a baseball bat and raised it to her shoulder. She didn't know how long the lock would hold out, but whoever crossed the threshold was about to add his face print to the frying pan.

The door opened a crack.

She tensed.

"Jessie?" Rick nudged the door the rest of the way.

She dropped her arms to her side and slumped as he stomped the snow from his boots before entering. "I'm here."

His gaze landed on the pan dangling at her side. He stuffed his back-door key into his pocket and cocked a brow. "Interesting weapon."

She shrugged, pushed off the wall, and returned the pan to the stovetop. She glanced over at the clock. Rick would never know there was a door behind it unless she told him. Part of her wanted to look inside for the first time alone but another part wanted to share the moment with him.

"This isn't a cartoon, Jessie." Rick hung his jacket on the hook by the door. "These people use real guns."

"I found a hidden door," she whispered.

Rick's eyes lit up. She had shown him the article, but he had scoffed at the idea. He had thought her dad would have known if there were any hidden places.

She pointed at the clock that concealed the door. "It's behind the clock."

Rick scurried up the ladder. "It's stuck."

"There is a release behind the right lip a few inches back from the edge. It's like a button."

Rick pressed the mechanism and swung the clock out

of the way. "Wow. I would never have guessed." His wide eyes glowed. "Have you looked inside?"

"Not yet. I just found it."

"There's no latch. Hand me a screwdriver."

Like a nurse aiding a surgeon, she passed him requested tools. In a few minutes, the door groaned open. "What's in it?" She stood on her tiptoes.

"Nothing." His posture sagged. He stepped down so she could climb up and see for herself.

Her heartbeat slowed to a dull thud. Heat built behind her eyes. She didn't find anything. The entire day was a waste. "Do you think burglars found it already?" Her words sounded thick to her ears.

"There are some gouges on the right. It looks like it was pried open at some point. Sorry." He leaned against the archway between the kitchen and the living room and finally noticed the rest of the house.

He gave a low whistle. "You've made quite a mess in here." He pushed off the wall and dragged the rug back to the center of the room, rolling it back into place with a kick of his heel. He moved the armchair back where it belonged with ease. No further questions. No judgment. No ridicule. Her ribs squeezed at his kindness. "I wish you would have found what you're looking for," he said.

Something deep inside turned at his words. Her heart seemed to pause, then pound. Blood rushed to her face, and her body temperature rose. She saw him with new eyes, and it set her skin tingling.

Jessie had been looking for someone like Rick all her life. Why hadn't she seen it before now? Rick was loyal, hardworking, and kind. She momentarily forgot about the house, the secret safe, and the possibility of a secret room. All she saw was Rick. The revelation disoriented her, and he stared at her strangely.

"Are you okay?"

She was better than okay, but she wasn't ready to tell him. She clamped her hands to her chest and stuffed her feelings inside. Suddenly nervous, she trudged over to the stack of pictures leaning against the wall and started rehanging them. She avoided his stare. "Do you have news about the case?" she asked.

Rick hesitated a second. He scratched his cheek and then rubbed the base of his neck. His eyebrows knitted together as he watched her. "Yes, Gavin located Rob downtown. He shoots the same rifle as the one used to target you. Rob wasn't willing to admit it, but his hunting buddies verified he was hunting in the area when you were shot at. It was enough for a warrant. Gavin is going to pick the gun up, and bring Rob in for questioning as soon as the warrant comes in."

She folded herself into the armchair. "Why would Rob target me?" She shivered as she remembered the hateful glare he gave her at Chenaniah Manor.

Rick dragged the couch back to its rightful place and sat across from her. "According to the officers investigating, his mom recently died. Provincial health coverage wouldn't cover all of her medical expenses, and Rob frequently verbalized his anger. He believes your dad stole his father's pension money, so he blamed him for his family's inability to pay for her alternative treatments. The time of your return was so close to his mother's death; it's likely what triggered his obsession."

"So, it was about my dad after all?" She didn't know whether to feel relieved or angry.

"This doesn't clear up the drug questions or tell us who killed Frankie, but once Rob is in custody, it should neutralize the immediate threat against you."

"If he's been trying to hurt me, could he have killed Frankie?"

"It's possible." Rick smiled sadly.

She wilted and lowered her chin to her chest. Could it really be over? She stared at her hands folded in her lap. She tugged one cuff of her sweatshirt over her fingers and rubbed at her eyes. Getting answers didn't provide her the elation she had expected. It made her feel like she had just lost Frankie all over again.

Rick reached over and placed a hand on her knee. "Now, about you searching this house alone." He smiled as if trying to lighten the mood.

Her cheeks burned.

"What if you would have found something today? What if it wasn't me at the door? Frankie's killer could still be out there. Rob still hasn't been apprehended. I want to be kept apprised of your plans, even plans like this." He gestured to the end tables that were still out of place from her search.

Her chin quivered, and she nodded. She heard the wisdom in his correction but still bristled at his command. "I'm going to Steadman's to borrow those diaries he told us about. You are welcome to come with me or stay here. It's up to you."

Rick snagged Jessie's arm as she stood to walk past. "I'm not trying to be difficult. Until we locate Rob, we need to be smart and stay safe. It's not a game."

She choked back a sob. "My brother's dead. Some wacko is trying to shoot me. Trust me. If this is a game, I'm playing to win."

Rick leaned in close. He hovered inches from her face, nose to nose. No anger in his expression. No frustration. Just concern. "Know what's even better?"

"What?" She swallowed the pain in the back of her throat.

"Not playing at all."

Jessie would not blink first. Seconds ticked. Finally,

she relented. "I just want closure." She brushed past him and snatched her jacket off the hook at the door. "We can deal with the rest of the house later. I want to get those diaries." She stepped out onto the porch ahead of him. She could hear him putting on his coat and commanding Max to guard the house.

As she walked towards Frankie's truck, a sudden need to be close to her brother, close to something that belonged to him, overwhelmed her.

"Jessie?" Rick called out to her.

She turned back to him.

A flash of orange lit the sky.

A thunderous boom and a blast of heat knocked her sideways.

Her face struck the cold ground. Debris rained as flames licked Frankie's truck.

Chapter 18

Rick dropped. He hit the porch as pieces of metal fell like arrows. A crazy silence followed. He tested his right leg, then left. Right arm, then left. Gingerly, he turned his neck from side to side. He'd live. When his eyes stopped bouncing inside his head, he focused on the glowing orange flames that ripped through Frankie's truck.

Jessie.

The contents of Jessie's purse lay scattered over the melting snow. A few feet from it, her still body lay in a crumpled heap.

No!

The memory rushed back, like a series of still frames. Jessie walked ahead of him as he locked the back door. He called her name. She looked at him. The blast. Her scream. The boom echoed in his ears. He hoisted himself upright and dragged himself toward the porch stairs. He heaved himself down.

A plume of smoke rose from the wreckage.

Sirens wailed.

A man stepped beside him and halted his movements. Where did he come from? He began the ABCs—airway, breathing, and circulation.

"I'm fine." Rick shoved back the Samaritan's hands and tried to stand up.

The man's lips moved, but Rick could hardly hear him. All he could hear was a constant roar. He shook his head. What was wrong with his ears?

"Jessie?" he yelled. He pushed away the man's hands. Why was he helping him? Jessie needed help. Not him. "Jessie!"

The man gestured for Rick to remain still. He mouthed more inaudible words but motioned toward Jessie. A woman bent over her. Was she doing chest compressions? Was Jessie breathing? Rick couldn't tell. *Lord, please.*

Another neighbor appeared with a fire extinguisher and sprayed white foam over the truck.

Rick struggled against the hands pressing into his shoulder. "Jessie!" Then Chief Brewer was there. If the chief had arrived, more time must have passed than he realized. Why couldn't he think straight?

"Rick, are you okay?"

Rick squinted at him. Why didn't he speak up?

Brewer mouthed some words to the Samaritan, who dutifully put pressure on Rick's shoulder. Rick looked at it with a strange detachment. Was he hurt? A small slice of metal protruded from his arm. Rick would have yanked it out if the blasted stranger hovering over him would give him some space.

Brewer rushed toward Jessie and dropped to her side.

The woman yielded to Brewer.

The neighbor stood just behind him, holding the empty fire extinguisher and blocking Rick's view.

Rick's head finally stopped spinning. He shoved the Samaritan's hot palms off his shoulder. Red seeped through his clothing. He yanked out the thick splinter-like chunk of metal and slapped his palm over the wound.

The chief's hands flew over Jessie's still body.

A wail clawed up inside Rick's throat. He'd failed Frankie. And now, he'd failed Jessie, too.

Firemen dragged hoses. Gavin pushed the growing crowd of neighbors back further.

Rick rose up, unsteady. "I'm fine," he insisted. He put his hand on the makeshift bandage Mr. Samaritan slapped on him and staggered toward Jessie.

Brewer blocked his path. "Let the medics work."

The medics. Rick hadn't noticed them arrive.

Brewer redirected Rick to the back of an ambulance and stood with him as the paramedics cut off his coat and shirtsleeve. The paramedic pressed a cold stinging cloth against the wound. Rick winced.

The medic released his pressure and examined the injury. "You'll be okay. Nothing else looks lodged in it. We'll butterfly it for now."

It dawned on him that he could finally hear again, but he didn't answer. His eyes remained fixed on Jessie. "Is she okay?"

"I don't know," Brewer said. What he didn't offer in words he made up for in his grim expression.

"Are you done?" Rick asked the medic. The man placed a warm blanket on Rick's exposed skin.

"Yup. All good. You might need a script for some pain pills tonight, and your coat and shirt are garbage. Sorry."

"I'll be fine." Rick stepped off the back of the ambulance and winced.

"You sure you're okay?" Brewer peered intently at him.

"I'm sure." He started toward Jessie, but Brewer redirected him again and guided him to Frankie's truck, now extinguished. "You're more help over here, not getting in their way. Tell me what you see."

Rick forced his attention onto the wreckage of the vehicle. "The truck should have been fully engulfed, but it wasn't."

Brewer nodded. "What does that tell you?"

"That a novice planted the bomb, or something went wrong."

Brewer led Rick around the vehicle in a circle. "What else do you see?"

Rick studied the vehicle, cinching his blanket tighter around his shoulders. "The front end is more charred than the back. We should search for the bomb closer to the front."

Brewer nodded again. "That's good. Specifically, where should we do our primary search?"

Rick pointed at what used to be the front right wheel. "I'd focus near the wheel well of the front tires."

Brewer snapped on a pair of latex gloves and handed Rick a pair. "Let's get to it."

The paramedics had strapped Jessie onto a gurney and were loading her into an ambulance. Rick froze, unable to tear his eyes away.

"This is how you can help her." Brewer spoke softly but firmly.

Gavin handed Rick a zippered sweatshirt. "Thought you might want a jacket. I let myself into the house and grabbed the first one I found."

Rick took it. It was an old one of Frankie's. Jessie had piled Frankie's clothes in the corner when she emptied some drawers. "Thanks."

"She have another break in? The house looks tossed."

"No, she was organizing." A burning sensation zipped through his chest as an image of Jessie holding that frying pan as a weapon filled his mind. She had prepared to fight him with spunk while the real villain was outside planting a bomb.

"Rick?" Brewer waited until he had Rick's attention.

Gavin took it as his cue to leave.

"It's time to catch this guy," Brewer said.

Brewer was right. Rick would find this guy and make him pay.

Brewer poked around the front end, which showed the most damage. He stooped to look under what remained of the frame. He reached out as if he was going to remove a loose piece of metal, and Rick shot out his hand to stop him. "Shouldn't the bomb squad do that?"

Brewer laughed, "We are the bomb squad. Welcome to a small-town force."

"Maybe we should call in the RCMP."

"We're not calling anyone. We can handle this ourselves." Brewer felt along the melted frame and pulled off a metal shard. "Bag this." He handed it to Rick.

Rick bagged it, and followed Brewer around the vehicle, cringing at his rough search. He felt for his phone. Somehow, it was still miraculously in his back pocket. He shot off a text message to Pete.

"I think we're done here." Brewer pulled off his

gloves. "Let's log this into evidence."

"Give me a minute. I'm gonna call the hospital and check in on Jessie."

The chief nodded.

Rick found a quiet space and called Pete, who promised he was mobilizing a plan to intervene.

"Don't get too invested in her." Pete cautioned him. If Pete wanted him to pull back and get some distance, it was too late.

Rick wasn't backing out now. Jessie needed him now more than ever.

He called the hospital. Jessie was stable, thank the Lord, but the mayor had put in a request that the police wait to question her. No officers were allowed in her room until tomorrow morning at the earliest. That included him.

Frustration slammed through him. He couldn't do anything at the scene, so he grabbed a clean shirt from the house and went to the station.

At the precinct, he pulled up the video of Jessie's attack in the police parking lot. They must have missed something. If Rob had attacked her in the parking lot, maybe the video held a clue that would help them find him.

He clicked on the correct video file and fast-forwarded to the approximate time when Jessie had parked her car and come into the station. The screen flickered and then went fuzzy. He hit both sides of the desktop computer with his palms.

"Come on." Nothing. A few minutes of fuzz and the video kicked back in and showed Rick and Jessie near the car discussing the note. He rewound it and played it again. The same thing. Someone had erased the recording.

"Rick. In my office. Now." Conrad's voice filled the room, and every eye turned to Rick. He felt the weight of their gaze as he made his way to the chief.

Rick had one foot in the hall and one foot in Brewer's office when the chief verbally tore into him. His voice carried through the open doorway where all eyes remained fixed on them.

"Care to explain why the RCMP has notified me they are taking over our investigation into Berns's explosion?" Brewer's eyes roamed over every inch of Rick's face as he stepped into Rick's personal space.

"I have no idea, sir." Rick shifted his weight onto his heels to force some space back between them. Pete had moved quicker than Rick had expected.

"Or why Pete Ryerse wants you on point, if you're available?" Brewer leaned in further closing the new gap.

The way he said it left no room for misunderstanding. Brewer suspected Rick and Pete had some connection, and it wouldn't take long for him to uncover their personal history—if he hadn't already. As soon as Brewer saw Pete, he'd recognize him as the man in the photograph taken in the hospital waiting room the night Jessie was pushed onto the ice.

Rick ground his teeth. "No idea, sir."

Brewer stared him down. A tiny muscle in his neck twitched. "I find it hard to believe that on the same day I reject your suggestion to bring in the RCMP, they're here of their own freewill."

Tightness gripped Rick's chest. It was impossible to diffuse Brewer's anger without reading him into the investigation, and that wasn't his call. It was Pete's.

"News doesn't travel that fast." Brewer clenched and unclenched his jaw.

Rick forced his expression to remain neutral and his posture to relax. He took another step backward. If Brewer backed him up any further, they'd be out of his office and in the hall.

"I'm happy to oblige them and take the lead."

"No, you're not."

"What? Not happy?" Rick shifted his weight on his feet, and the office doorknob jabbed into his back.

Brewer leaned in, eyeball to eyeball. "You're not taking the lead on anything. As of this moment, I'm putting you on leave."

Rick pushed off the wall switching instantly from defensive to offensive. "You can't do that."

"I can't prevent the RCMP from investigating, but I

am absolutely within my rights to handle my team of officers as I see fit. You're too close to this. You have a personal relationship with Jessie. You need to get some distance. I suggest you go home."

"Distance? You can't be serious. Reassign me if you have to, but don't cut me out."

Brewer returned to his desk and stood in front of it. He folded his arms across his chest and tapped his index finger on his bicep. He nodded his head to indicate that he expected Rick to take a seat.

Rick sat.

"You're on leave, as of now, for insubordination."

A million objections raced through Rick's mind. If he wasn't on the force, he couldn't protect Jessie. He couldn't look into the attacks. He wouldn't know anything. How was he going to save her if Brewer cut him out? "That's not fair. I've done everything by the book—"

Brewer leaned in. His freshly mouth-washed breath made Rick's gut recoil. "I know you've been tracing her ancestry and quietly investigating a case I told you was closed. No paperwork requesting that we officially reopen Frankie's death has come across my desk. You've wasted a lot of time on this, and I have given you a lot of room, but now you are dangerously close to going rogue—if you haven't already."

Brewer's hand landed on his shoulder, giving him a

slight squeeze. "This is for your good."

Rick shook his hand off.

"You can't see that I'm right because it's true. You're too close," Brewer repeated. "Jessie needs someone with a clear head, who has a firm grasp of the facts, not an emotionally driven friend. It's too similar to Sarah. I don't want to see a good career ruined."

"Sarah?" Her name tasted bitter on his lips. When would that woman's choices stop defining him?

"You have to admit; there are similarities." Brewer ticked off points on his fingers one by one. "Two women. Both needy. Both convinced you are the only one that could save them. After Sarah, you needed to prove yourself. Prove you could do this. I understand, Rick." Brewer's voice softened, "You're not the first officer to go through something like this."

"This isn't about Sarah or about proving myself." He had to stay on the case.

"No, it's not about Sarah, and it's not about Jessie. Not anymore." Brewer held out his hand. "Your badge and gun. Now."

A wave of nausea washed over Rick. He stripped himself of the two things that defined his life and slammed them down onto the table instead of putting them into Brewer's hands. "You're making a mistake."

"I could say the same thing to you." It wasn't victory

that filled Brewer's eyes. It was sadness. Over what? Cutting Rick out? His role in the drug ring? Did Brewer have a part in the bomb? Rick couldn't tell.

He left the office in a daze. Who was he if he wasn't a cop?

Chapter 19

Jessie peeled open her gritty eyelids. What time was it? She pushed herself up on her elbows. Early morning dimness illuminated shapes in the hospital room that the blackness of night would have concealed. It must be near morning.

Rick exhaled a gentle snore, his large body twisted into an inadequate bedside chair. Had he been there all night? His head tipped against the chair back and his mouth hung open. She pushed herself into a sitting position. The sound of her bedsheets rustling shot him upright.

"Are you okay?" He immediately scanned the room. The storm raging within his gaze calmed the second their eyes met. Three deep creases in his forehead smoothed, and he scooted his chair closer to her bed.

"How long have you been here?" She licked her lips. Her tongue felt like sandpaper.

He picked up a plastic tumbler of water and held a drinking straw to her lips. "I slipped in as soon as Steadman left." He set the cup down and scooped up her hand. He carefully avoided touching the area connected to an IV bag.

The way he caressed the palm of her hands in smooth long finger strokes sent shivers tap dancing up her spine. Her pulse throbbed in her wrist, but he gave no indication that he noticed her increased heart rate.

She wouldn't deny the physical attraction between them any longer, but it didn't mean she had to act on it. Rick worked for the RCMP. And she lived at least ten months out of the year on the road. Not exactly a match made in heaven.

She tugged her hand free and plucked at the bedsheet. She wasn't ready to admit the pleasure his presence gave her. "Shouldn't you be processing the scene or arresting someone? I'm pretty sure a bomb went off." Her awkward attempt to lighten the mood fell flat when she struggled to adjust her position on the bed, and her chuckle morphed into a wince.

Rick pitched forward and slid an extra pillow behind her back. "Is that better? Can I get you anything?"

He could give her a lot of things but not the things she wanted. She wanted her brother back. She wanted a dad who was invested in her life. She wanted answers. And, if she were totally honest, she wanted more than brotherly affection from him. She shook her head. Pain shot through it.

His gaze followed her every move. It wasn't fair. Detectives were trained to read expressions. She wasn't ready for him to know her inside and out. What if he learned the very worst about her and walked away? She wasn't sure she could survive another loss.

She pretended to untangle her IV lines. "I thought Chief Brewer would have you all over the town looking for clues, not babysitting me. Unless—" Her heart thumped, and the monitor beeped at the spike in rhythm. "Are you guarding me?"

A nurse swept into the room and checked the monitor. She pressed a button. "You need to remain calm. If your company gets you too worked up, we'll have to limit your visitors."

Stay calm? Easy for her to say. No one had tried to kill her recently.

Jessie smiled anyway. "I'll try."

The nurse gave a stern look to Rick, made a note on her chart, and left.

When the nurse was out of earshot, Rick dropped his voice to a near whisper. "I think it's safe to assume that until we catch whoever is behind this, you're in danger. Rob is still missing. But, no, I'm not guarding you. I'm, ahh—" He looked up at the ceiling and sucked his bottom lip into his mouth. "—temporarily suspended."

Her jaw went slack. Suspended? How long had she been unconscious?

Rick rubbed his knees with his palms. "No badge. No police weapon. Not an officer right now. Just a friend visiting a friend."

His attempt at nonchalance didn't fool her one bit. Moisture brimmed her eyes. Losing a job would be painful for any man, but losing one that defined you—this had to be killing him. "What happened?"

"The chief thinks I'm too close to you to be objective. He thinks my inability to distance myself might be hurting you more than helping you."

There was more. She could tell by the way he didn't hold her gaze. Funny how quickly they had come to read each other's nonverbal signals. "What else does the chief say?"

"He figured out that I have been investigating Frankie's case, even though it is officially closed."

"Oh, Rick—"

"And that I had something to do with Pete and the RCMP showing up after the bomb."

"You called in Pete? Won't that blow your cover?"

"You're more important than my cover."

Elation filled her heart even as she blinked back tears.

He smiled and stroked her hand. "But I was able to

250

maintain it."

"And it cost you your badge," she choked out. She could only imagine how a power-hungry alpha male like Brewer responded to Rick going above his head and calling in the RCMP.

Rick forced a brighter face. "What have the doctors said about you? Are you here for an extended stay?"

"I'm certainly racking up the frequent flyer miles." She studied her folded hands in her lap. "The doctor said I'm really lucky, but cheating death this many times doesn't make me feel lucky. It makes me feel hunted." She lifted her head and focused on his face.

Rick pressed his lips flat. "We're going to figure out what's going on."

She never doubted it. But would he be able to do it before her luck ran out? "How? You don't even have your badge anymore."

"Not everything needs a badge. For instance, a badge would have prevented me from sitting here all night. Beth and Steadman earned you a few days without police questioning. Apparently, it pays to be related to the mayor."

So, he had been here all night. Her insides somersaulted. She didn't know what to say. "Did you find anything at the scene?"

Rick hesitated like he doubted her ability to handle

anything more.

"Don't you dare hold back on me now. I am a lot stronger than I look. Even the doctor said so."

His eyes crinkled at the corners.

It set off another explosive, this one inside of her.

"The car bomb was amateurish. Set off by a remote."

"That's good, right? That means we should be able to catch them? Amateurs make mistakes."

"And someone erased the tape of your dad putting the note on your car and you getting attacked in the police parking lot."

"Why? What does that mean?"

"That means whoever is behind this has access to the police records."

"So, it's not just Rob." She sagged against the pillows. It wasn't almost over. Not by a long shot. This was bigger than Rob seeking revenge.

"Everything is connected, sweetheart. We just don't know how yet."

Her face warmed at his endearment at the same time her insides cooled over confirmation that the police force was dirty.

Rick rested his elbows on his knees with an expression that was a mixture of disappointment and hope that reminded her of Max when he didn't get his daily walk. "They can force me out of the station, but they can't force my brain to stop working. If we work together, we'll figure this out. I know we will. Frankie had too much information on the town history, the building and closure of Eastmore, the defeat of the previous mayor, and the establishment of Steadman's social programs to be mere curiosity on his part. Something bigger has to be at play."

"How far back does this drug ring go? Frankie was investigating Eastmore and Steadman. Could his digging have ticked off the wrong person? Could Steadman be involved? How does any of this connect to Eastmore's closing?" She didn't expect all the answers. She just needed to voice the questions.

"When you returned to town, you found some college kids messing around the property. Somehow, in the scuffle, you picked up the missing drugs."

"Maybe that's what they were looking for? Maybe they cleaned out the safe behind the clock but dropped the bottle that somehow landed in my purse?"

Rick sat up straight. "What if they didn't find all the drugs? That would explain why someone keeps coming back to the house."

"And to the kennel. I was pushed onto the ice because I interrupted someone poking around the kennel."

"And then things escalated. Poisoning you at the funeral was not reactive. It was premeditated."

She shivered. "Do you think it was Rob, or someone

else?"

Rick shook his head. "Rob wouldn't have known about your allergy, so I think we are looking for two people, at least."

"Two people with a grudge against me. One wants me out of the house—or at the very least—off the property and the other wants to hurt me."

"If we didn't move Max from the kennel into the house to guard it, who knows how many more times they would have broken in?" Rick said. "We can't know how many attempts the dogs have hampered.

Jessie could have never anticipated how thankful she'd become for Max's company when she first arrived. They started leaving Max along with Duke and Daisy patrolling the property every time she left the premises. Duke and Daisy weren't quite as intimidating as Max, but they weren't the Welcome Wagon either.

"Jessie?" Dr. Smith and his nurse swept into the room. "Your test results came back fine. I'll get a nurse in here to unhook your IV, and you'll be discharged."

"Wonderful news, isn't it?" the nurse chirped. "You're very lucky only to suffer cuts and bruises after such an explosion. Should I call the mayor to come pick you up?"

"I'll take her home," Rick said.

Going home didn't sound so great when someone wanted her out of the house bad enough to kill her.

Jessie's fingers hovered over her laptop keys. Her computer rested on her lap. A makeshift office was spread around her on the couch. She should be working on her article for her editor, but she couldn't focus. Not while some crazy person was looking to off her.

Rick pounded away on his computer following up leads. He sprawled in the armchair across the room from her. She didn't want to write about the Winter Diamond Festival. She wanted to do something, anything, to help Rick figure out what was going on, but she didn't have any more information on her case.

Maybe she could help Rick with his demons?

Ronald Anderson.

It might be nothing. It might be everything. She plugged the reporter's name into the Google search bar. Most of the hits were online article links. She scrolled through pages and pages, skimming the article titles. She clicked a link that contained an image of Sarah. The woman looked nothing like Jessie had envisioned. Her long blonde hair, trim figure, and beautiful features didn't line up with a girl desperate for attention. Jessie couldn't help but compare her mass of dark curls to Sarah's fairer features.

She clicked back to the search feed and perused a few

more article titles. Anderson had done some serious reporting in his earlier days. Why would he resort to writing such trash about Rick? Most writers aspired to move from the tabloids into serious journalism, not the other way around. She clicked through the links to his social media accounts. She scrolled through pictures and newsfeed updates.

Bingo! Sarah's beautiful face was on Anderson's page inside the album titled: *Summer Holidays*. "Hey, come take a look at this," she said.

The sofa sagged as Rick joined her on the couch.

"That's Sarah, right? With Anderson." She pointed out his profile picture.

Rick scrolled through the pictures and read the captions. *Cousin fun. Sailing with the family.* "They were related?"

She nodded. "It makes sense. It's the only thing that would explain the way he nosedived his career to start reporting such sleaze on you. No wonder he won't let up."

"That does explain his relentless approach," Rick agreed. "But it doesn't change anything. She's still dead because of me." He pushed himself off the couch and returned to his computer.

Rick was right. This didn't solve anything. She got up, and her stiff muscles screamed at the movement. The doctor may have given her the all-clear, but her bruised body disagreed. She relocated her computer to the kitchen table where Frankie's family research was spread out.

She plunked the kettle on the stove. "Want some tea?"

"Sure." Rick followed her into the kitchen and flipped through the papers on the table. "What's all this?"

"Some of our family history that Frankie had dug up."

Rick picked up a paper. "Wow. It says here that your Grandpa James married into money and his new father-in-law was concerned about Grandma Maggie's husband squandering her inheritance. So along with the dowry, he sent her with a diamond instead of cash. The projected worth of that diamond today is nearly a million dollars." He let out a low whistle.

Max came running.

"That wasn't for you." He scratched behind Max's ears.

Jessie reached into the cabinet and removed a dog treat. She tossed it to the floor. "Here you go." Max settled down with the rawhide snack.

"The legend says that people suspected Maggie also doubted her husband's integrity because she never wore the diamond. Rumor claims that she hid the diamond somewhere on their property." Jessie explained.

Rick looked up. "This is the original house, right? The diamond could be here?"

"I guess so, yes. When the historical society

challenged the building of the factory, Eastmore agreed this property would remain untouched. It was situated far enough away from the factory that it didn't affect their plans."

The kettle whistled. She plunked two mugs on the counter and scrounged around for tea.

"Let me get that." Rick took over.

She surrendered the kettle and opened the kitchen island's lower cabinet and reached for a box of cookies. A mouse scampered over her slippered foot.

"Oh!" The cookies slipped through her fingers and scattered across the floor. She toppled onto her backside.

Rick lunged to catch her and missed, knocking the mug off the counter.

"Ow!" She rubbed her hips and pushed the broken shards of pottery away from her.

Max lifted his head, considered the cookies, and went back to chewing his rawhide.

Rick offered her a hand up. "Are you okay?"

"No," she groaned. "Where there is one mouse, there are two. And where there are two, there are many." She crinkled her nose. "I hate mice."

Rick guided her to a chair and carefully picked up the shattered mug. He wiped up the spilled water and then pulled out every pot, dish, and pan from the cabinet, piling them in the sink. When the cupboard was finally emptied, he used a dustpan and a small broom to sweep up the mouse droppings. Half of his body disappeared into the large cabinet. "Frankie must have some traps around here," he called out.

"I'll look." She handed him a disinfectant cloth to wipe out the base and started opening and closing cabinets. Where would Frankie keep traps?

"Ouch!" Rick banged his head on the underside of the countertop.

"You okay?" She peeked into the cabinet.

"There's something sharp down here... a piano hinge? I can barely see, but I feel a breeze coming up through it." He looked back at her, amazed.

This was it! The secret room! Her pulse quickened as Rick pulled up on the bottom of the cabinet and a door lifted on the hinge. Concrete stairs disappeared underneath the house into a dark tunnel. It was just like Aunt Norma's magazine had described.

Body aches forgotten, Jessie grabbed her phone for a flashlight and dashed ahead of Rick.

He heaved her back out by the waist. "You follow me." His tone left no room to disagree.

She grabbed a heavy belted sweater with deep pockets and followed Rick into the awkward opening. After descending a few steps, she closed the hinged trap door above her. Instantly, darkness cloaked them.

"Watch your head," Rick said. He turned on his phone light app and swung it back and forth in an arc.

She stooped to avoid knocking her head against the low ceiling. The temperature dropped as each step moved them deeper underground. She copied Rick's movements with her phone light, and their combined beams lit up the musty space. "This is unbelievable," she whispered. She didn't know why she whispered. It just felt right.

She grazed her hand along the rough mud-caked walls as they walked. The dirt floor sent frozen icicle daggers through her feet and into her legs. Her slippers weren't thick enough to ward off the cold, but she didn't want to complain, or Rick might insist they go back for her shoes.

Rick forged ahead. She couldn't see his face, but his breathing was raspy and short. Despite the cooler temperatures, her insides heated. She strained to see into the darkness that stretched beyond the lit arc of their phones.

"You okay?" Rick paused.

"I'm a bit claustrophobic." Her muscles resisted obeying the commands of her mind. Her chest tightened.

"We can go back."

She shook her head. She could do this.

"I can keep looking and tell you what I find."

No way was she going to let him have all the fun.

He leaned one shoulder against the wall and hovered

nose-to-nose with her. His moist breath heated her face. He moved like he was about to speak, frowned, and looked down. His hand seemed to disappear into the wall, and he pulled out a book.

She shone her light on it. "It's a journal! Like the ones Beth found."

"It's a hole dug into the wall." He reached in again and pulled out a clear plastic bag of pill bottles.

Jessie shone her light directly onto the bottle labels. "Fentanyl, OxyContin, Demerol," she read. "And look at these names, Stan Broadwick, Pat Green, Stella Freeman. These are all residents of Chenaniah Manor!" She looked up at Rick. "Stan isn't taking his meds. That's why he is in so much pain!"

"I knew Chenaniah Manor was at the heart of this," Rick said. "Frankie must have hidden them here after he called me, along with the diary. Will these fit into your pockets?"

She stuffed the bag into one of the large pockets on the front of her sweater.

"Why wouldn't he have put these into the clock safe?" Ricked wondered.

Jessie shrugged. "Even when he was a kid, he hid things in several spots. He'd have multiple stashes of Halloween candy all over the house. That way if I found one, the rest were still safe."

A scraping sounded a few feet ahead. They froze.

Who else would be in the tunnel? Is this how those men got in and out of the house those times? Rick put a finger to his lips, and they clicked off their light apps. Darkness descended.

Chapter 20

Rick couldn't quite tell if the soft muttering was an actual voice or the groaning of the earth.

A pinpoint of light grew larger as he and Jessie crept forward. As they neared, words became clear and more easily heard. Someone was definitely at the other end of this tunnel.

He pulled Jessie to his side, and they crouched together. They peered through a loose slat in what appeared to be a hidden doorway that opened into the kennels.

Rob Green paced across the room, flicking a Zippo lighter off his thigh. Rick couldn't believe it. The man the entire police force was searching for was muttering to himself on the other side of the flimsy wood. Rob circled five cans of gasoline stacked in the center of the room.

Jessie's sudden inhale tickled his ear.

Rick's heart hammered in his chest, and he held his

breath, but Rob did not hear them above his muttering.

Rick pressed his hand into the small of Jessie's back. "You have to get back to the house," he whispered. He pulled out his personal weapon. Sounds of splashing liquid and the scent of benzene burned his nostrils. Rob was going to torch the place.

"She's gonna burn. Gonna burn the house down. Gonna burn," Rob chanted.

Rick tugged Jessie back toward him. Rob said *she*, not *it*. And he said *house*, not *kennel*. If Jessie was the target, not just this building, he couldn't send her back to the house alone. She was safer with him.

Jessie tensed under Rick's hands. *"The dogs,"* she mouthed.

Daisy and Duke paced in their kennel. The yipping of the other dogs rose to a frantic pitch as they sensed something amiss. The hairs on Daisy's neck raised upright, and a warning growl rumbled from Duke's throat. The dogs recognized this man as a threat.

Rick's fingers flew over his phone's keypad. *Get to the Berns kennels – fast. Send fire trucks. Rob's here.*

Rob stomped around splashing gasoline onto the walls, floor, and furniture. Every time his jacket flapped open Rick caught a glimpse of a gun in his belt.

"Rick," Jessie hissed. "We can't let him hurt the—"

Rick clamped his free hand over her mouth, pushing

her back against the wall.

Her eyes widened in fright.

He didn't mean to scare her. "Not another sound," he whispered.

"Who's there?" Rob spun toward the noise and crept closer to them. "I heard you."

Rick stood nose to nose with Jessie, close enough to see her pupils dilate despite the darkness. Her lips trembled against his palm.

"Where are you hiding?" Rob kicked open cabinet doors and splashed more gasoline around. "Come out or burn."

"Get ready," Rick mouthed to Jessie. He removed his hand, and she licked her lips. She nodded.

As soon as Rob turned his back to them, Rick broke through the slats with his gun trained on the man. "It's over, Rob."

Rob spun and flicked open the lid of his Zippo in one fluid motion. "It's not even close to over."

Rick circled around, so his back was to the doorway. Behind him, Jessie clung to the fabric of his shirt.

"Why?" Rick asked. Help might arrive in time if he could keep Rob talking.

Rob's arm, holding out the lighter, dropped slightly as he gestured to Jessie. "If her dad hadn't taken our money, we could have treated Mom. Maybe then... then," Rob's voice caught. He jerked his arm up again and struck the lighter wheel with his thumb. A flare licked up with a hiss. "She deserves worse than this," Rob's tone hit a deadly low. "Her dad took everything from us. So, I'm gonna take everything from her."

Rick clicked the safety off on his gun. "I'm not going to let you do this."

"You're not gonna shoot me. I know how you cops play the game. You're not in personal danger. You can run out that door anytime. Your job is to talk me down." Rob knocked the lighter lid back down with a flick of his wrist, extinguishing the flame. He flicked the lid open again. He taunted them, "Will he, or won't he..."

Jessie's fingers relaxed their hold on the back of his shirt.

"Hey, get back from there!" Rob struck down on the wheel again and ignited a new flame.

Rick jerked his gaze toward Jessie, who now crept along the wall. She reached for the release button that would open the exterior kennel doors, so the dogs could get outside.

"Stop it!" Rob spun back toward Rick with a wild look in his eyes. He yanked the gun from his waistband.

Rick didn't blink. He squeezed the trigger. The gunshot rocked the room. The bullet caught Rob in the shoulder and flung him backward onto the tabletop. The

Zippo, still lit, dropped to the ground and ignited the spilled benzene.

"Jessie!" Rick screamed.

She had dashed to the panel box rather than the exit.

"Jessie!" The flames zipped up the trail of gasoline and set the curtains ablaze. They shot up the fabric to a metal shelf and spread out like a mushroom in search of more fuel.

"Got it!" Jessie slapped the release to free the dogs and their kennel gates automatically opened into the fenced yard. She turned back towards Rick as flames reached the gas-soaked floor in front of her. A wall of fire burst upward.

"Rick!"

A chill raced down Rick's spine. He snatched a blanket off the nearby cot and raced to the sink to drench it in water. He threw it to her, over flames that burned steadily at waist height. Ripping a fire extinguisher off the wall, he shouted, "When I blast it, cover yourself and run through!"

The smoke had already filled the top third of the room, devouring the breathable air with each second. In a few more minutes there would be no air left.

"I can't!" she screamed.

He yanked the pin out of the extinguisher and aimed the hose at the base of the flames that blocked Jessie from the exit. As he squeezed the lever, a powerful shot of foam exploded from the hose. He swept the spray from side to side. He'd never be able to put out the growing fire with this, but he might be able to clear a path. "Run!"

She wrapped herself in the wet blanket and dashed through the smothered flames. As soon as she cleared them, she threw off the blanket and ran right into Rick's arms.

He dropped the extinguisher and spun her toward the exit just as the firemen ran in. Help had arrived.

Spray burst from a hose as another fireman ushered them outside. They collapsed onto the lawn, and a paramedic rushed over.

To the right of the building, an ambulance waited with flashing lights. Another paramedic was treating Rob's gunshot wound. Rob must have crawled out during the chaos.

Rick rose unsteadily to his feet. Rob could have killed Jessie tonight.

He took a step in Rob's direction, hands fisted at his sides. Jessie rested a hand on his shoulder. "Let the police do their job," she whispered.

The chief blocked Rick's path. "She's right. It's not worth it. We caught him as he was running out." Brewer's gaze dropped to the gun tucked into Rick's holster. "I thought I took that from you?"

Rick stiffened. "It's my personal weapon."

Brewer opened his hand. "Since you discharged it tonight, I'm going to need you to turn it over to me."

Rick's hand rested protectively over his gun. If he hadn't had it tonight…

"It's okay," Brewer said, reaching out for the gun. "It's over. We got him. He made the bomb. He set the fire. It's done."

Rick surrendered his weapon.

Jessie swayed as Brewer's words registered, and Rick gathered her into his arms.

She buried her face into his shoulder. "Is it really over?" She trembled.

The smell of smoke rose from her hair. Rick had come close to losing her tonight. Again. He tightened his arms and planted a kiss on her temple.

"This part is over," he whispered.

Rick finally got a call into Pete to report.

"Stan Broadwick, Pat Green, and Stella Freeman," he read the names off the various pills bottles safely secured inside a plastic baggie, thankful he'd stashed them in Jessie's sweater. They could have been destroyed in the fire.

"Are they all residents of Chenaniah Manor?" Pete asked.

"Every one, and their prescriptions provide quite the smorgasbord of drugs." He listed the drug names. "I didn't turn them over to Brewer, and Jessie never mentioned them to him in all the excitement."

Jessie rolled over on the couch where she rested. The poor girl had to be beat. He didn't understand how she could be soft and feminine one moment and tough as nails the next. But she was. She risked her life to free the dogs from the fire. Part of him wanted to scold her for endangering herself, but another part was incredibly proud of her bravery and compassion. He was falling in love with her, and if Pete found out, it would cost him his job.

He stood at the kitchen window. A few remaining firemen monitored the final stages of extinguishing the fire. "What do I do about the pills?"

"Hold onto them until you can give them to me," Pete said. "We still don't know who can be trusted on the force."

"What about Chenaniah Manor? Brewer suspended me."

"Yeah, but I didn't," Pete said. "You work for me, remember?"

Adrenaline rushed through Rick. "Then I'm heading to Chenaniah Manor tonight."

"Try not to blow your cover."

As Rick ended the call, Jessie roused from where she rested on the couch.

"I'm coming with you," she said, rubbing her eyes as she sat up.

"Not a chance." With Rob in custody, Rick no longer feared sniper shots, but it was still better that Jessie remain here, away from the impending showdown. "The firemen will be here for a while. You'll be safe with them just outside."

"You're shutting me out?"

"I'm doing my job."

It took Rick over an hour to convince Jessie to stay at the house. By the time he arrived at the retirement home, darkness had begun to creep over the streets. Chenaniah Manor's owner, Derek Bommel, would be leaving soon. He waited outside in his car.

At five minutes after six, Derek exited the front doors with his brother Sam and one of Sam's dogs. He nodded at the people he passed, perfectly playing the role of the kind neighbor.

Rick opened his car door and got out. As Derek paused to cross a street, Jessie emerged from a nearby coffee shop, her eyes trained on Derek.

Rick slammed the car door. When would that woman ever listen?

"Derek!" he called, drawing the man's attention away

from where Jessie stood to watch their exchange.

Derek spun at the sound of his name.

"I have a few questions for you." Hopefully, the news of his suspension hadn't reached Derek yet.

"This isn't a good time." Derek tugged his coat around him tightly.

"We could head to the station," Rick bluffed.

Sam tugged up on the dog's leash, and it immediately sat at his heel. Derek pulled a hankie out of his jacket pocket and dabbed at his sweaty forehead despite the chill in the air. "What's going on?"

"It's come to my attention that residents have been mishandling their prescription drugs."

Sam narrowed his eyes. "How does that connect with my brother?"

Rick braced himself. He could take out Derek no problem, but without a weapon, two on one might be a bit harder.

Derek shifted his weight from foot to foot as he waved his hands. "It's nonsense. Our residents are lovely people."

"Who are grossly undermedicated." Rick darted his gaze to Jessie who was approaching from behind the men.

"I can speak with the nurse—" Derek began. He shifted his eyes as if looking for an escape and chewed his bottom lip.

Rick steered them into a nearby alley, away from

innocent bystanders on the street.

"How exactly is this connected to Derek?" Sam scratched his eyebrow and scrunched his nose.

"Because of this," Jessie spoke from behind, holding up a photo of the baggie of medication with labels naming the residents. She must have printed it at home.

"You shouldn't be here," Rick growled.

"Frankie is my brother. He died because of this drug scheme. I deserve to be here." She stepped toward Derek and handed him the photograph.

Derek's hand trembled.

Sam's eyes darkened as he looked at the picture over Derek's shoulder. "I knew you were up to something. I knew there was more to you pushing me to buy Frankie's business."

It suddenly made sense. Derek was buying medication from the residents. That's why Mr. Broadwick was hesitant to ask for pain meds. He'd already sold the prescription. Derek pushed Sam's interest in the business to gain access to the property to try and find the missing drugs, and when Sam didn't succeed in the purchase, Derek broke in to search.

Derek's countenance shifted as if he could tell Rick had fit all the pieces together. He narrowed his eyes and glared at Sam. "If you weren't so weak-willed, you could have pressured her to sell when she first got here, and then

I'd have been able to search her place without all that sneaking around. But no, your bleeding heart backed off."

The dog growled at Derek but remained seated by Sam's heel. Sam tightened his hold on the leash.

"You think you're so smart," Derek seethed. "You think reinventing yourself after Eastmore closed makes you special. It doesn't. We all reinvented ourselves. We had to. We were losing everything."

"What did you lose?" Sam tightened his hold on the dog's leash. "You had your apartments filled."

Derek threw his arms into the air. "No one could afford to move into Chenaniah Manor after Berns stole their pensions, so I promised them what they deserved, their money."

"How many were being prescribed medications they didn't need to offset their rent?" Jessie asked.

Don't draw his attention, Rick wanted to scream.

Derek turned his wrath toward Jessie. "Your brother messed the whole thing up. He came to see Sam and happened to be wearing a sweater like mine. Then that old man gave his prescription to Frankie. We then decided to pin the entire racket on him, but then you showed up, yipping about his cleaned-up life and new ways."

"Frankie was clean," Jessie whispered. "I knew it!"

"Your family deserves everything they get." Derek lunged at her, clamping onto her arm with his meaty fingers.

Jessie yelped. She twisted her body, and Derek snagged her necklace. The stones scattered with loud pings.

A guttural snarl emitted from Sam's dog. Sam looked to Rick for permission.

Rick shook his head. If Sam turned his dog loose, Jessie might get hurt.

Rick lifted his hands in front of his body in mock surrender. "No one has to get hurt today. Let her go."

Derek wrenched Jessie's arm harder.

The dog lurched, but Sam yanked him back. He dragged him out of the alley.

Jessie stumbled, throwing Derek off balance.

"Gun!" Rick shouted. He dove at Derek, wrestling for control of a weapon that had suddenly appeared in his hand.

A shot echoed in the alley. Rick, Jessie, and Derek hit the pavement, and all were momentarily still.

Rick raised himself to his elbows to relieve Jessie of his weight. Her scrunched up eyes eventually relaxed. She finally cracked open her eyes, and their gazes collided. Foreign emotions pounded through him and he felt more in that half-second their gazes tangled than words ever could have verbalized. He knew, whatever happened from this point on, that this brave, dynamic, and intelligent woman had changed him forever.

She shifted underneath him. He pulled her away from

Derek.

Derek writhed, rolling himself onto his stomach as he stretched out his hand toward his gun, which had landed just out of his reach when they fell. A small baggie of pills lay on the ground beside him.

Sam ran back toward them. He kicked the gun toward Rick and dropped to his brother's side. He rolled him over and put both hands on his shoulder, applying pressure to stop the bleeding. Derek yowled, but Sam never let up.

"He was going to shoot you," Rick whispered into Jessie's hair.

She turned toward his voice, stiff and pale, already displaying the early stages of shock. A person didn't just bounce back from everything she had gone through today.

"We need to get you warm." He'd have given her his shirt, but the damp fabric stuck to his upper arm where a deep crimson spread through the cotton fibers. The bullet had grazed him in the struggle. He scooted backward until his back pressed against the wall. He winced, pressing his hand against his right tricep, sending hot daggers shooting through him. He'd been hurt worse before. He'd be fine.

Jessie sat beside him, and they surveyed the scene together. She lifted her blood-covered hands, turning them in front of her face.

"Are you hurt?" Rick asked.

"It's not my blood." As she said the words, her eyes

widened, finally seeing the growing stain on his sleeve. It rocketed her out of her daze. "You've been shot!"

Jessie pressed her hands over his fingers, adding more pressure to the injury. Blood oozed through their combined fingers.

He gritted his teeth. "I'm fine. It's just a flesh wound." The fear on her face ripped through him worse than the bullet. He didn't want to cause her any more pain. He closed his eyes. Sirens sounded. Someone must have called the police.

She lifted his arm to elevate it above his heart.

Gavin burst onto the scene with two medics close behind. "Are you okay?" he asked Rick.

One paramedic dropped to Rick's side, and the other ran over to Derek.

The medic examined Rick's wound. "Went right through. Should heal nicely." He glanced up at Jessie while he worked. "This is a switch. You're usually the patient."

"I can't say that I like being on this side of the experience any better." Her hand trembled where it rested on the back of Rick's neck. Something about the way she worried about him warmed him.

"Better me than you," Rick groused. "I've been shot before."

Jessie paled even further, and the paramedic paused in his treatment on Rick to study her face. "Don't go into shock on me, Miss Berns, or you *will* become the patient."

"Oh, my phone!" Jessie pulled her phone out of her pocket. "I recorded everything." She pressed stop. The recorder must still have been going.

Pride surged through Rick. "Atta girl." He had to admit, they did make a pretty good team. "Nancy Drew and the Hardy Boys are in for some serious competition."

She smiled.

Rick looked toward Gavin, who stood over the paramedic checking out Derek. "Is he gonna be okay?" he called to the officer.

"Yeah, just banged up a bit," Gavin said.

"Cuff him as soon as he's stable," Rick said. "He's behind the drugs. There might be others involved."

"Who else?"

"He didn't say." Rick glared at Derek. "But he will."

"You have the right to remain silent," Gavin began.

"The dog!" Jessie suddenly lurched forward. Sam's dog was chewing on a clear bag holding more pills. It was the baggie Derek had dropped.

A second gunshot shook the alley.

Rick grabbed the back of Jessie's shirt and yanked her to the ground. Pain shot through his arm again as the length of her body landed hard on his.

Gavin slowly turned, his gun hanging limply at his side.

The paramedic beside Derek's crumpled body sprang into action. His partner raced to his aid. A large puddle of darkness began to seep out from underneath the fallen man. His head rolled to the side, and a trickle of red streamed from his mouth and nose.

The medics' hands stilled.

Brewer rounded the corner as the medic pronounced him dead.

"What's going on?" Brewer roared.

Everyone started talking at once.

Rick stood to his feet and swayed.

"He shot Derek—"

"The dog had the drugs—"

"I only turned away for a second—"

Gavin remained frozen. Rick approached him like he would a cornered animal, his good arm outstretched in front of him, nonthreatening and cautious. He removed the revolver from Gavin's hand. Police officer or not, it was never easy to take a life.

Rick handed the gun to the chief.

"When I took your service revolver and badge, Rick, I didn't imply you could go all cowboy on us."

"I know." Rick wasn't about to apologize.

"He had grabbed another weapon," Gavin babbled. "I looked away for a second, and he was aiming at Jessie—"

"We'll get it all sorted out," Brewer promised.

279

Chapter 21

Three days later, Jessie descended the staircase of Frankie's house in a floor-length gown. The look in Rick's eyes and the way his jaw dropped sent the good kind of shivers down her spine.

"You're stunning," he said.

She didn't own a formal dress, so she had visited one of the specialty shops downtown to prepare for the Diamond Ball, the highlight of the Winter Diamond Festival. The saleswoman steered her away from the standard black most women favored and instead brought her this deep blue sleeveless sheath that nipped in at her waist and dusted the floor. The saleswoman gushed at how the color warmed her complexion, but Jessie had doubted her sincerity, considering the hefty commission she was bound to pocket after a sale. However, Rick's reaction proved the saleswoman was spot on, making the expensive gown worth every penny.

"Aww, you wore your good sling." Jessie gently nudged his bandaged arm. Her stomach somersaulted at the touch, and she fumbled to cover the moment. "The black looks great with the tux."

Rick smiled until his gaze fixed on the table, where the newspaper lay. A frown wrinkled his forehead. "You saw it."

She picked up her clutch purse and double-checked that she had tucked her EpiPen inside. "What? The newspaper? Pfft." She tossed it into the trash. "We know Anderson's problem is personal and, one day, so will the rest of the world."

His face contorted in controlled anger.

She ran a finger along his flexed jawline, and it relaxed under her touch. "You saved my life. You broke a major drug ring. You're a hero."

A smile replaced his frown as Rick slipped his hand under her elbow and steered her toward the front door. He held it open for her. "I've been called worse."

"You shoveled the snow with only one good arm?" Frankie's snow shovel lay against the house, and a path to Rick's car had been cleared.

He grinned. "I couldn't have you walking through a foot of snow in killer heels like those."

Pleased he'd noticed her shoes, she accepted his arm

and let him guide her to the driver's side of her newly returned car like Cinderella to the carriage. Technically, since the threat against her was gone, she could have driven herself to the ball, but they had slipped into this wonderful habit of traveling together. And despite his unwillingness to admit that his sling made managing the car tricky, he needed a chauffeur. After all he had done for her, she was pleased to fill the role.

He closed her door and walked around to his side. A contented sigh slipped out of her. She would miss this when she left Chenaniah River. If only Rick would give her a reason to stay. If only it were possible to merge their lifestyles.

"We never did finish our diamond hunt," he said when he climbed into the passenger seat. "Are you disappointed?"

She turned the key, and the engine roared to life. She didn't care as much about the unfinished hunt as she did about the unfinished kiss.

He reached across the console and played with a tendril of hair that had slipped from the loose knot she had styled it in. How on earth she was supposed to focus on driving when he did stuff like that?

"Had we finished the hunt," Rick said as he curled her strand of hair around his index finger, "we'd be stuck standing in line waiting for it to be appraised. Now we can spend the night dancing."

Her nerve endings tingled. She liked the sound of that.

A crowd filled the ballroom to capacity, and the line to the appraiser wound all the way around the perimeter of the room. The dance floor held only a handful of couples keeping step to the soft music played by the live band. Rick was right. They'd have more fun without the diamond.

Rick twirled her onto the dance floor with his good arm, and a peal of laughter bubbled from her. His eyes lit up at the sound. Was she crazy to hope that he no longer thought of her as his friend's kid sister? He pulled her close. She rested her head on his shoulder. If only this moment could last forever. He tipped his head down and whispered into her hair, "Did you get enough info for your article?"

Like the screech of an off-key violin, he had sucked the romance from her heart. He was all business. Or all big brother. It didn't matter which. Both left her out in the cold.

"Yes, I think I did." She pulled back, creating a bit of distance between them. Coolness swept in, and she prayed it would reduce the embarrassing red that had to be flushing her burning cheeks. When would she learn? She'd thrown herself at him enough times to know that his presence in her life was as a surrogate older brother not as a romantic partner. She tipped her head to the side. "How does it feel to break the biggest drug ring in Chenaniah River?"

His lips lifted into a half smile. "Pretty good."

"What I can't figure out is why a nice old man like Mr. Broadwick would be part of the drug scene ruining our youth," Jessie mused.

Rick tugged her a bit closer. "When we interviewed him, he said all the seniors believed Derek was funneling the meds to senior citizens in other cities who were in worse shape financially than them. They didn't see any downside."

Jessie scoffed, "Except that it was illegal—"

Rick cut her off by twirling her around with astounding ability considering his injury.

"So, the window, the break-in, that night on the ice, the allergy attack…" She shivered. "…that was all about searching my property?"

"As far as we can tell," Rick said. "There are still some things left to figure out." Rick spun her again.

"Like what?"

"For starters, if Derek killed Frankie, why did Frankie greet him as an officer?"

She pulled her lip into her mouth and considered it.

"Why, or better yet, how did he erase the recording of your dad leaving that note? And who pushed that pottery off the balcony at Chenaniah Manor? Derek's alibi placed him near the front desk." Rick's brow furrowed most adorably. He snuggled her closer as he talked out the unanswered questions like he wanted to protect her.

A woman wearing more business attire than formal wear waved at Rick. Jessie felt his sigh more than heard it.

"You should talk to her." Jessie pulled out of his arms until only their hands remained connected.

He gave her an incredulous look.

"If you don't, she'll get the story another way." Jessie gave him a small push in her direction. Sooner or later, she was going to have to let the undercover world have him back. Goodbye was coming. It might as well be now. "Go. Redeem your reputation. I see Steadman and Beth. I'll visit with them."

He grabbed the tips of her fingers before she could break their contact. "Jessie—"

She forced a smile. "I'll meet you back here in fifteen minutes."

"Promise?" he asked.

For a second, the hard veneer she had been trying to wrap around her heart cracked. "There's no place else I'd rather be."

She felt Rick's eyes following her as she hurried away. As much as she wanted to confess the feelings she always had for him, she traveled for a living. It would never work. He saw her as a sister. A few weak moments wouldn't change that. If she wanted to leave Chenaniah River with the all the pieces of her heart intact, she'd do good to remember that.

"Detective Chandler, your name has been in the news a lot lately. What can you tell us about the recent claim that you've put another woman at risk?" The reporter pressed a microphone up to Rick's mouth, and a bright camera light shone in his eyes.

Rick tried to keep a sight line on Jessie, but the dancers kept getting in the way. "The case is ongoing, so I can't comment."

"Can you confirm that you saved Jessie Berns's life?"

"Who told you that?" Rick strained his neck around the dancers. With the bright camera lights and the dancers constantly moving around the floor, it was impossible to see anything. There! A break in the crowd showed her approaching Steadman, who stood by the art display featuring Frankie's work.

The reporter didn't answer Rick's question. She pressed on. "I have a source that says in a split-second decision you took down the suspect before he was able to raise his weapon at Miss Berns. Is that correct? And…" She looked briefly at the notes on her phone. "Isn't it true that the woman whom Anderson claims died under your watch was taking advantage of her connection to you, and that you didn't ignore her call the night she died as the reporter had stated? You were, in fact, saving another woman and her child from an abusive situation."

Rick snapped his full attention to her. "Where did you get that information?"

The reporter smiled and lowered her voice. "Off the record, I'm a friend of Jessie's. In exchange for an exclusive interview, she told me about Anderson's relationship with your informant."

Jessie put a woman and child in danger? His eyes roamed the room, but he didn't see her.

The reporter went on as if she still had Rick's full attention. "Jessie and I did a bit of digging and uncovered Jane and her child. They're safe. Her husband was brought up on unrelated drug charges. A judge recently sentenced him to a lengthy prison term."

Rick inhaled his first full breath since Jane and her daughter had gone into hiding. They were safe. He could finally speak against Anderson.

"Jessie wants to clear your name and make sure the world knows you're a hero," the reporter whispered expectantly.

Admiration filled Rick. Jessie really would make a good investigative reporter. And now on live television, her friend was here to help him redeem his name, painting him as a hero, as the man he always wanted to be. The kind of man Jessie deserved.

A bell rang, and the room sprang into applause. A disco light descended from the ceiling and bounced flashing lights off the walls. A few dozen balloons fell from a suspended net. The appraiser had identified the real diamond.

"Looks like they found their diamond winner." The reporter momentarily swung her attention to the stage. As the cameraman swiveled his light in that direction, Rick caught a glimpse of Jessie and Gavin studying one of Frankie's photographs.

Except Gavin studied Jessie, not the picture. Jessie stepped closer and peered intently at the image. Gavin moved beside her, leaving no space between them. He cupped her elbow and led her into an adjacent hall.

A waiter stopped in front of them and offered them a beverage. Gavin took a glass of sparkling water and pressed it into Jessie's hand.

Rick wracked his brain. Where had he seen this waiter before? The lanky man's eyes darted all around the room, and Rick's gut clenched. This was the guy in the photographs the chief had shown him, the dealer from the college campus drug crimes.

Gavin nodded to the waiter and placed his hand on the small of Jessie's back and ushered her around the corner. His wife, Kenzie, stood off to the side and watched, appearing unconcerned that her husband was guiding an attractive woman away.

The reporter maneuvered herself into Rick's line of sight. "Is there anything you'd like to say to the people who have been slandering you?"

"I'm sorry, but I have to go." Rick shoved the microphone away and forged a path across the dance floor to the last place he had seen Jessie.

"What kind of man doesn't want to clear his name?" she called after him.

We, Derek had said when he spoke of the drug ring. Frankie called the man *officer*. Gavin had too much money. The shaggy looking man from the campus photographs looked an awful lot like the waiter. The threat against Jessie wasn't over—not by a long shot—and he had allowed her to come here tonight with her guard down.

He paused at the photo that captured Jessie's attention. The focal point was the town square. Many people bustled about, but in the background, Gavin, Derek, and the waiter were huddled together. Rick leaned in and looked closer. They were exchanging a package. Gavin was the inside man.

Rick spun on his heel as Kenzie, Gavin's wife, sashayed over. She threaded her arm through his and tried to steer him toward the dance floor. "Come on, Ricky. Dance with me," she purred.

"Not now." He untangled his arms and jogged around the corner. "Jessie!"

Voices came from a room off to the side. Rick drew a gun out of his sling, thankful Pete had outfitted him with a weapon through the RCMP. He peeked into the room. Another door stood open at the back. Gavin was manhandling Jessie in that direction.

"I won't tell anyone, I promise!" Jessie pleaded.

Gavin cupped her cheeks and pinched her mouth open. He sloshed the water down her throat, spilling it over the front of her dress. "You couldn't leave it alone, could you?" Gavin gripped her with one hand and dangled Jessie's purse just out of her reach.

Jessie fought against him. "Let me go!" Then, her eyes widened. She clawed at her throat. She lunged wildly for her purse.

Her EpiPen! They had spiked the water.

Jessie retched and fought Gavin as Brewer emerged through the back door behind them.

Rick slipped into the room and trained his gun on Gavin.

"I'd put that away if I were you, Detective Chandler." Brewer extended one hand in front of him with his other hand hovering over his gun. "You're still on leave, remember?"

Gavin spun around. "Chief?"

"What's going on?" Kenzie entered from behind, startling Rick with her question.

"She's having a reaction," Gavin said, dropping Jessie's purse and releasing her. "I was just going to get some help. No need for guns." He stood slowly with his arms raised.

How long did Jessie have? Rick's eyes bounced from Gavin to the chief to Kenzie. Who was the greatest threat? Where was Shaggy?

Gavin's hands moved toward his hip.

"Hands where I can see them!" Rick shouted. "Jessie, are you okay?"

She moaned and fumbled for her purse.

Gavin's eyes flicked behind Rick.

The hairs on the back of Rick's neck stood at attention.

Brewer whipped out his gun and leveled it at Rick.

Rick swallowed against the vomit that shot up his throat. Not the chief, too. He shifted his position and alternated his gun between Gavin and Brewer. "Chief," he said thickly.

Gavin moved.

"Rick—" Brewer roared.

Rick squeezed the trigger at the same moment a bullet burst from Brewer's gun.

Screams filled the adjacent ballroom.

As the chief rushed past him, Rick charged forward

and shoved a howling Gavin down. He pulled zip ties from his sling. He grimaced as pain shot through his injured arm while restraining Gavin.

He had to get Jessie's EpiPen. He lunged toward Jessie and took her purse from her fumbling hands. He emptied the contents on the floor.

Gavin's gun had skidded across the floor, stopping near them.

"Did you find the pen?" The chief struggled with Shaggy who bled near the doorway where Rick had been standing. Brewer zipped Shaggy's hands together. His gruff manner held little sympathy for the writhing man who had snuck up behind Rick.

Rick didn't answer the chief.

The click of heels on the floor gave him pause. He looked up.

Kenzie had an odd look on her face. She made a sudden move for the gun near Jessie.

Rick dove for the gun, knocked it away. He rolled onto his back, pointing his weapon at Kenzie's chest from his position on the floor.

Jessie closed her fingers around the EpiPen, snatching it from the dumped-out contents and administered the drug. "What did you try to give me?"

"Try?" Rick's mouth hung open.

"I didn't swallow," she said thickly. Her words

sounded as if her tongue had swollen from the exposure, but thank the Lord she had not swallowed. It bought her some time.

Sirens wailed outside. Screaming and chaos momentarily increased as the main doors burst open and the RCMP invaded with their weapons out.

Brewer roared, "Everybody put the guns down!"

"Who called the RCMP?" Rick asked.

"I did," Brewer explained as he picked up Gavin's service weapon. "As soon as I saw Frankie's picture." He tied Kenzie's hands

He nodded toward Rick's gun. "How many of these am I going to have to take away from you?"

Rick hesitated, "Ah—"

Brewer smiled. "It's okay. It's over."

Pete tipped his head toward Jessie as his RCMP team took over the scene. "Officer Gavin Thorn, you're under arrest for drug trafficking, money laundering, attempted murder, and the murder of Derek Bommel."

"I'm not taking the fall for this," Gavin ranted.

"Not to worry. There are enough crimes to go around." RCMP officers hauled Kenzie and Shaggy off to be formally charged.

"How did you figure it out?" Rick pressed a kiss to her temple inhaling her sweet lilac scent.

"The picture. I saw them in the background of

Frankie's picture."

He pulled her in close. "Nancy Drew has nothing on you."

Tears wet her cheeks. "You ripped your stitches."

Rick rested his chin on the top of her head. "Why did you go with him so easily?"

She buried her nose in his shirt and inhaled. "He shoved what felt like a gun into my side. He said he'd shoot you if I didn't."

A spotlight landed on them, broadcasting their moment to the world. Jessie's reporter friend and her cameraman hadn't evacuated with the crowd but had followed Rick, capturing the entire arrest scene on tape. The reporter looked ecstatic at her career-making luck.

Brewer was right. It was over.

Chapter 22

"Do you think you can restring the pendant? It has special meaning to me." Jessie held her breath as the jeweler laid the river stones on a black velvet cloth draped over a small tray.

He examined them one by one under a magnifying glass. Fred's Jewels had been serving the people of Chenaniah River as long as she could remember. However, Fred Jr. ran the business now.

Jessie stole a glance at Rick, who watched Fred closely. She couldn't believe Rick had gone back to the alley and found every single stone from her necklace. How he differentiated between her river stones and general rubble, she didn't know. He said there was something about the feel of the stones.

"Where did you get these?" Fred turned the stones over in his fingers.

"It's a Berns family heirloom," Rick said. "Why? Is something wrong?"

Fred didn't answer his question. He scooped up the tray holding the stones and relocated to the back counter near a microscope. He placed one stone onto the microscope slide and looked through his eyepiece at the bottom of it. He examined each of them. "Have you noticed these engravings? There is something etched on the bottom."

The jeweler stepped back and invited Jessie to look through the microscope. She pressed her eye to the lens. There was something there.

"I might be able to magnify it more." Fred twisted a few dials and knobs and looked through the lens again. "There. Look at this."

Jessie motioned for Rick to have a peek through the scope. "It looks like coordinates of some kind, but I could be wrong. Do you have a piece of paper?"

Fred handed him a slip of paper, and Rick scratched out some numbers and letters. "P, L, E, A, P, 25."

"I'm not sure if this will help decode your message," Fred said, "but the stones are also fairly distinctive."

Jessie frowned. "They just look like regular river stones to me."

"They are a unique composite. The only area in these parts where you can find this kind of stone is on the property of the old factory."

The old factory was the also the old homestead. The letters and numbers must mean something. Had the mystery of her family, the mystery Frankie had been trying to unravel, been around her neck this whole time? Her eyes flicked to Rick.

Rick reached for her hand. "We'll figure it out," he promised.

Hours later, they had retreated to Frankie's house and were no closer to solving the mystery than before. "I think we've tried every combination," Jessie groaned. She flung herself onto the sofa and rubbed her eyes. "My brain hurts."

Rick scratched his temple. "Is Nancy Drew giving up?"

She shot him a dirty look. "If we are going to keep working, I need caffeine." She walked to the kitchen and measured out coffee to brew.

Rick dragged his hand down his face. "What was that picture at your uncle's house? The one Daisy painted."

She placed two empty mugs on the countertop. "It was an apple tree gone wild. Why?"

"That diary we found in the tunnel belonged to Daisy. It had an apple embossed on the cover." Rick leaned forward and fiddled with the letters again. "Look at this." He held up a piece of paper. "APPLE 25."

Jessie forgot about the coffee. She plucked the paper

from his hands as her mind spun. She closed her eyes and pictured the painting hanging in Steadman's home. "You can just make out the old front porch through the painted tree branches." She snapped her eyes open. "That's it."

"What?"

"If we counted off twenty-five steps from the front porch, do you think we'd end up under the tree?" They locked eyes. A slow smile spread across his face. This had to be it.

Armed with shovels and hope, they counted off twenty-five paces from the porch and ended up under one of the many old apple trees that had been part of an orchard she'd long-since forgotten about. After a lot of hard digging into the frozen ground, Rick's shovel clanked against metal. "Hey, I've got something."

Jessie bent down and used the blade of her spade, carefully scraping away the dirt covering a metal box. She ran her hand reverently over the top of the case before lifting the handle and heaving it out of its frozen grave.

"Open it," Rick urged.

She tried to lift the lid, but the hinge was rusted shut. She rattled and pulled the hinge. Nothing worked.

"Let me try." Rick took the box and used the tip of his shovel to pound it open. A few good strikes, and it popped, spilling out some old papers.

Jessie snatched them up before the snow dampened the

pages. "It's a family tree of some sort." She flipped a page over. Nothing was written on the back. She handed it to Rick and started reading another one. Her eyes glistened, and her voice trembled. "This was what Frankie was looking for."

Rick studied the second document over her shoulder. "Did you see this?" He pointed to some legal jargon at the bottom. "It says there is a deed to a piece of land."

They picked through the box and Jessie reverently lifted out a faded document. She scanned the page and covered her mouth with one hand. "This goes from Frankie's property all the way to the factory."

Rick read over her shoulder. "Wow."

She felt lightheaded as she lifted her face to Rick's. "I own this?"

"I think you do. Did you notice the name?" Rick leaned over and pointed out the title.

The paper trembled so violently in her hands she could hardly read the text: "Diamond's Edge." They had finally solved the mystery of the lost diamond.

A foot crunched on the snow behind them.

Jessie turned as Beth slammed a shovel into the back of Rick's head and knocked him unconscious.

"Rick!" Jessie dropped to his side. She ripped her gloves off her hands and felt for a pulse. A faint throb beat under her fingertips. *Thank you, Lord!* She couldn't take her eyes off Rick even though Beth still wielded his discarded shovel.

"It's mine," Beth exploded. "Give me the diamond!"

Beth had watched long enough to know they found the "diamond," but not long enough to know it was a deed, not a stone.

"It was Steadman's legacy!" Beth seethed. "All these years, all this time looking for heirlooms to build up our family name and you tumble into town, and we are supposed to lose it all?"

Rick groaned.

"Get up." Beth nudged Jessie with the tip of the spade. "We're going for a walk."

Frankie's research collided in Jessie's brain as Beth prodded her from behind. "You began looking for family heirlooms when Steadman began his run for mayor," Jessie said. "But your research uncovered that he wasn't the rightful heir. You ran Dad out of town so you could keep the inheritance. How did you pin the pension loss on him?"

"I worked on the legal team for Eastmore. I found the loophole that allowed the company to close and forfeit on the underfunded pensions."

"If it wasn't illegal, why did Eastmore hide it?" She fingered her phone in her pocket. She felt along the familiar raised buttons and pressed what she hoped was the recorder.

"Eastmore knew public backlash and court cases would come when the news of the underfunded pension hit the papers. It could halt the sale. Pinning it on your dad gave me the chance to solve two problems at once."

"You ran us out of town while saving Eastmore the bad press," Jessie finished.

"It was our legacy. We built this town. You've never done anything for Chenaniah River," Beth spat her words. They were nearly at the river.

Jessie spun to face her attacker.

Beth lifted the tip of the shovel and pressed it against Jessie's chest.

"When Rick mentioned my inherited allergies came from Dad's side of the family, Steadman told you, didn't he? You pieced together that Dad had to be back in town for Rick to know that."

"I thought I saw him one day, but I couldn't be sure. It looked like he was with some officer."

"That's why you sent Rick that text on my old phone. You pushed that planter off the balcony. You wanted Rick there. Then Dad would find out and come to Chenaniah Manor to make sure I was okay. Then you'd know where he was."

"I ran your family out for a reason. And my secret was safe until Frankie started poking around."

"You found my phone on the river bank, didn't you?"

"I held onto it until I could use it. It was easy, and it worked," Beth smirked.

"You won't get away with this. The police will tie you to this."

"No, they won't. I took the diary you found. It's the only proof that you're the heir. The police will assume you met with another unsavory person from the drug trade, especially considering all that recently transpired. When I tell them I found you floating face down in the river and ran to the house to phone for help, I'll also say I stumbled across Officer Chandler's body, who tragically died trying to defend you."

She had to keep Beth talking. *Please, God, wake Rick up!* "How did the legacy get so twisted over the years?"

As if she was finally pleased to discuss it openly, Beth boasted. She lowered the shovel slightly. "At some point, one of Steadman's uncles twisted the legend. The inheritance has always run through the daughters, but this uncle terrorized his sister, who was too weak to challenge him. Since no one knew where the actual diamond was, she let it go. It wasn't worth the fight. Her diary explains it all."

"So, Steadman honestly believes he is the heir?" Jessie hardly dared to hope. She wouldn't be able to stand it if her cousin was in on this from the very beginning.

"Steadman has no idea what I've done to protect his legacy."

A branch snapped behind them.

Beth spun toward the sound.

Jessie pounced on her back. She wrapped her arms around Beth's neck and pulled tight.

Beth swung the shovel like a wild woman, and they tumbled to the ground.

Then, Rick was there.

Like he always was. Like she always wanted him to be. He gently pried her fingers off Beth and used his scarf to bind Beth's hands. "It's over, Jessie. This time, it's really over."

Rick leaned his shoulder against the wall outside of Brewer's office where Jessie gave her official statement to the Chief and RCMP.

Jack paced between closed office doors. "Now this is all settled; she'll be safe, right? She can return to work?"

Jack's question pierced through Rick. Jessie's future wasn't in Chenaniah River. "She can travel if she wants to travel."

A satisfied smile spread across Jack's face. "That's all I ever wanted, her able to do the thing she loves."

"Well, I hope she plans to stay." Steadman joined them. Once it had become clear that he had no part in his wife's scheme, he was released. He clapped Jack on the back. "It's time we had some more family around here." Steadman's joy over clearing Jack's name couldn't conceal the lines of grief carved by his wife's deception. A cloud of sadness hung over him despite his happy words toward his cousin.

"And I am finally free from that safe house?" Jack and Steadman turned to Rick.

He nodded.

Relief flooded Jack's face. "The way you've been guarding me I was beginning to wonder if I'd ever get out."

Jessie, Brewer, and Pete exited the office.

"All that matters is that Jessie is safe." Steadman pulled Jessie into a quick side hug then released her. She immediately embraced her dad.

"And that Frankie didn't steal, sell, or use any drugs." Jack looked pointedly over Jessie's shoulder at Brewer.

"Chief Brewer was close to solving the drug ring," Pete said. "He couldn't absolve Frankie without tipping his hand to Gavin." Pete looked at Rick. "That's also why he didn't trust anyone, especially a new transfer to the department."

"I knew someone on the force was dirty," Brewer said.

"We finally pieced everything together. Frankie was clean. He had no part in this." Jessie leaned into her dad. Exhaustion lined her face.

Rick wished he could scoop her up and bring her home, but she needed the closure that piecing all the details together would provide.

"We found Frankie's missing inhalers at Shaggy's, along with an old police uniform and the missing drugs." Brewer directed the group into a conference room where they all sat down around a long table. "That supports Jack's story of an officer watching Frankie die. We suspect Gavin outfitted him."

"Shaggy, whose real name is Thomas, deals drugs at a university campus and drives a gray compact vehicle with a Free the Animals bumper sticker on the back," Rick filled in. "That's why he had Gavin erase the surveillance tape of Jack putting the note on Jessie's car. So she wouldn't recognize the car." He folded his hands on the table and looked at Jack, who sat across from him beside Jessie. "Thomas was inside the vehicle when Jack left the note. He was also the one who attacked her in the parking lot."

"I saw Thomas's car again outside the church after the funeral." Jessie placed her hand on her dad's and squeezed.

"Right," Pete confirmed. "While Derek kept you occupied, Gavin snatched your purse and ran it out to Thomas, whom Rick later ran out of your house."

Rick's gut twisted at the memory of how close Jessie came to facing Thomas alone. Thomas was a violent man.

"Gavin was using his clearance at the station to

misplace evidence that could link back to them, and he used his position to obtain a city truck. The GPS put on your vehicle came from our supplies too." Brewer looked directly at Jessie. "I'm truly sorry, Ms. Berns."

Jessie nodded in acknowledgment. "Thomas was at the house the day I arrived in town. He was in the mix of college kids trying to set the dogs free."

"We think he started the puppy mill rumor as a cover," Rick said. "While the animal rights people released the dogs, he searched the house for the drugs and the incriminating photograph. When he was finished, he turned off the electric fence and let Max out to keep his cover as one of the activists."

"And I had already collected Frankie's pictures for the art show," Steadman said. "So, Thomas wasn't able to find what he was looking for."

"Right," Rick said. "He specifically wanted the picture that showed Derek, Gavin, and Thomas in the background handling the drugs." Rick studied Jessie. Despite looking exhausted, she appeared to be holding up okay.

Jack furrowed his brow. "But there weren't any drugs at the house, and Thomas had Frankie's phone. Wouldn't the picture have been on it?"

Jessie shook her head. The lines around her eyes deepened. "No, Frankie doesn't use his camera phone for pictures. He favors manual cameras. Besides, they needed to eliminate the picture entirely."

Jessie was starting to fade. Rick needed to wrap things up. "When Gavin learned that some pills turned up in Jessie's purse, Thomas admitted that he had found a couple of bottles that night in the safe behind the clock, but since he didn't find the entire stash they were looking for, he pocketed them to sell privately. He had dropped the bottle that Jessie stumbled across on her arrival."

"I'm impressed." Jessie lifted her exhausted gaze to Rick's. "How did you find me at the river with Beth?"

"I used the Find Your Family app Daniel had installed."

"I think it's time to go home. You coming, Dad?" Jessie stretched her hand toward her father.

"Me?"

"Yes, Dad. It's time to come home.

Chapter 23

Rick reclined on the couch with Jessie. She had tucked herself under the shelter of his arm. She wrapped her hands around a steaming mug of coffee and smiled up at him with complete trust. He pulled her closer, loving the way they fit together. He was crazy to hope for many more nights like this. Their paths were not traveling in the same direction. She'd be off on a new writing adventure soon, and who knew where the RCMP would send him next. Brewer had offered him a job here, but without Jessie, the town held no appeal.

"Dad, I'm so sorry I doubted you," Jessie sniffed and pulled the cuff of the sweatshirt she had changed into over her hand and rubbed her nose. Rick loved the way the sweatshirt hung off one shoulder, all cozy and soft.

Jack's eyes filled with appreciation. "I'm just glad it's over. Really over. And I'm looking forward to getting to know my daughter again."

"Me too." Her eyes softened.

Rick tightened his arm around Jessie and snuggled in. His throat grew thick. This could be the last time he held her. His voice cracked, "What are your plans now, Jack?"

Jack scratched the back of his head and stared into the fire.

Max looked up from where he lay on the rug, curled in front of the warm flames, and then rested his head back onto his paws.

"I don't really have any plans." Jack looked sheepishly at Jessie. "I was kind of hoping to move back in here, but I don't want to intrude."

Jessie's eyebrows lifted. "Of course, you can live here. I still have my apartment in the city. There is no point in this place sitting empty, and then we don't have to rush through sorting all Frankie's things."

So that was it. She was returning to the city to keep traveling the world writing stories about her adventures. Rick adjusted his position, shifting her away from him. She leaned forward and set her drink on the coffee table and repositioned herself at the opposite end of the sofa.

She smiled at him, and it awakened places in his heart he thought had died. But she was leaving. What did he expect? He had nothing to offer her that could compare to her jet setting life. He stood to add another log to the fire and poked it with the fire iron. As oxygen hit the embers, flames shot to life. "What does it mean now that you're the diamond heir? That sounds pretty huge."

Jessie shrugged and tucked her feet underneath her. "Steadman is the town leader. I have no desire to change or challenge that."

"Maybe not," Rick shrugged. "But you can't change that you're the star in the fairy tale this town has built a festival around. You're like a Valentine Princess."

"Or the Diamond Princess," Jack laughed.

Jessie groaned and threw a pillow at her dad. "Don't use those words in front of Steadman. He's already looking for a way to spin this and I have zero desire to be known as a princess."

Jack deflected the pillow, and it landed near Max who lifted his head and plopped it onto the cushion. "You'll always be my princess," Jack said.

Jessie groaned again. "Maybe after I read all the diaries, we'll find new skeletons in the family closet." She changed the topic brilliantly with a Nancy Drew kind of glint in her eye.

"Hold it right there." Rick recognized that trouble making twinkle. "I just solved one mystery, a pretty big one at that. Even the Hardy Boys took a day off now and then."

He hung the fire iron back in its stand and dusted his hands on his thighs. "I've got a few things to do, and since you two have some catching up to do, I'll head out now."

He extended a hand to Jack. "It was a pleasure to work with you, Mr. Berns."

Jack gave it a firm shake. "Thank you for everything. You didn't just solve Frankie's murder; you gave me back my life."

Rick nodded.

Jessie walked Rick to the door. She wrapped her arms around her middle. "When will I see you next?"

"Unless you need me in the kennel, I should start sleeping at home." His stomach heaved at the idea of being so far away from her. But if she was going back to the city, it was time to make a clean break and say goodbye.

"You know," Jack interrupted, following them into the kitchen. "I'd love to learn how to care for the dogs. Could you show me? Maybe train me before you go?"

Rick's stomach dropped like an anvil. Now that it was clear he and Jessie had no future, he was eager to make his exit.

"Do you want to take over the business?" Jessie's voice rose with surprise.

"Sam and I have been talking," Jack said. "He and Frankie were talking about a partnership, and it might not be a bad idea."

Rick rubbed his chin with his thumb and forefinger. A few days. That was all it should take. "Okay. I can show you everything," Rick promised.

Jack followed Rick onto the porch. He latched onto Rick's arm and prevented him from descending the steps. "Can I give you a little fatherly advice?"

Rick nodded.

"I learned the hard way what happens when a man lets pride ruin his life. I wanted to clear my name. I wanted to prove to Frankie and Jessie that I wasn't a thief, but my ego was too injured to return and face the town people and fight for it. Maybe if I had, Frankie wouldn't have died. Maybe Jessie and I wouldn't have all these lost years to make up." He held Rick's gaze. "Don't make the same mistakes I did. Don't let pride win."

Rick frowned. He had convinced himself that letting Jessie go was what she needed, but maybe it wasn't. Could pride be the only obstacle between him and his future?

Never did she expect her life to turn out like this. She had her dad back, learned she was an heiress, and sent a family member off to jail.

She pulled her vehicle into the driveway and removed her phone from her purse. She was ready to make the call. Finally. As the engine idled, she dialed Sam and left him a voicemail. "Thank you for your offer, but we won't be selling Frankie's dogs after all. Our family is taking over the business." Family. She liked the sound of that. "However, we are interested in discussing a possible partnership. Give me a call back, and we can set up a meeting for me, you, and my Dad."

Dad trotted around the back corner of the house, and half-a-dozen dogs nipped at his heels. The puppies were larger now and behaved like toddlers in need of constant attention. Dad tipped his fur-lined hood her way, and she grinned. Who would have thought her dad would resettle in Chenaniah River and keep Frankie's business alive?

She held up a finger to communicate she'd be another minute before coming inside. It was time for one more phone call. Her article on the scandal of Chenaniah River's Diamond Heir made national news. Rick's live rescue captured by Channel 4 cleared his name and redeemed his reputation. And this morning, she signed a book contract to write the full story. Agents were already circling and talking about movie rights. She had one year to complete the assignment. She called her magazine.

Her editor answered in her usual clipped and hurried voice.

"I'm giving my two weeks notice. I won't be returning to *Travel the World with Us*."

Sure, she was sad to close that chapter of life, but she was ready to put down roots on the same land her ancestors had.

An image of Rick flashed in her mind. She shoved it aside. She needed to be thankful for what she had. There was no sense longing for what she couldn't have. Undercover officers didn't get married, have kids, and lead normal lives.

She worked out her exit strategy with her editor and disconnected the call. She would have never written her ending this way. Not in a million years. If she had penned her ending, the heroine would have found the hero and lived happily ever after. But if she learned anything through all of this it was that her story wasn't really her story to tell. It was God's story. And God was writing something much bigger than she could have ever dreamed. That was the story she wanted to tell. That was the story she wanted to live.

She got out of her car and stomped through the snow toward the porch. As she rounded the sidewalk, a large structure hidden under a tarp came into view. She frowned. It wasn't there before. Taped to the front was a note. *Remove me.*

She looked for her dad, who watched through a parted curtain from inside the house. He winked and let the curtain slip back into place. She approached the tarp, almost shyly. What was Dad doing?

She tugged at the cover, and it slid off. She gasped. A

pile of stones.

Her hand automatically went to her neck, where the pendant once laid heavy but was now bare. How did Dad know?

Wait. There was something on the landscaping stones. She moved closer to the memorial. A date was engraved on each rock with a few words underneath: Dad's return date. Frankie's sobriety date. Her salvation date. Rick's vindication date. Her rescue dates. Romance.

Romance?

She squinted. Today's date.

She inhaled his familiar woodsy scent before she heard Rick's footsteps crunch in the snow behind her.

"This is your reminder." Emotion roughed up his voice. "It's your reference point. Every time you face a new trial, a new adventure, a new unknown, you can look here and remember the God who never walks away from you."

Rick moved close, so very close. The air between them vibrated with energy. "I don't know what tomorrow brings," he said, "but I know that I love you, and I'll love you every day for the rest of my life if you'll have me."

Her mouth gaped open.

He raised his hands. Dangling from a silver box chain hung her pile of stones necklace pendant.

"You restrung them?" Her heart somersaulted. She pressed a hand to her chest.

"May I?" He lifted the necklace, and she obediently turned around. He clipped the chain around her neck letting his fingers graze her skin. She leaned into his touch.

She stroked the smooth stones and spun back to face him. "When?"

"I had Fred tell you the police took the stones into evidence, so I could surprise you."

Her eyes filled.

He knelt down and planted his blue jean clad knee in the snow. Her hands cupped over her mouth. This couldn't be… no, it couldn't.

"Jessie Berns," he paused.

Her heart pounded in her throat.

"Will you be my Nancy Drew?"

Laughter bubbled up from her toes, dissolving the emotional tension in her chest. "What?"

"Chief Brewer offered to keep me permanently on staff. So—" He pulled a ring out of his pocket and, just like that, the vice grip on her lungs was back. "I can't think of anyone else with whom I'd rather fight crime, right wrongs, and raise kids."

She dropped to her knees in front of him and gently nudged the ring down, so there was as little space between them as possible. Her words blew across his lips like the foreshadowing of a kiss. "I've always wanted to marry a Hardy Boy."

Acknowledgments

Fatal Homecoming is the product of many brainstorming sessions with my writers' group – thanks to both Karen's in our group, Sandy, Sandra, Tara, Hunter, and Heather. It never ceases to amaze me how our little group can take an idea and run with it until it becomes a story.

A special thank you to Rick Ryerse, Pete Chandler, and Ken Van Noort. Your expertise and experience in the police force, in the RCMP, and as a paramedic made the life-threatening scenes of Fatal Homecoming come alive. Any mistakes in depicting these scenes are mine.

Thank you to Write Integrity Press, Marji Laine Clubine, and Angela Maddox for polishing the story, and to all the members of my launch team. I had a BLAST getting this book off the ground, and your enthusiasm was a joy.

If you enjoyed Fatal Homecoming, please consider returning to its buy page to leave a review for the author.

About the Author

I am from the *play-until-the-streetlights-turn-on* and *come-when-your-father-whistles* generation. I'm a cool-off-in-the-sprinkler, drink-straight-from-the-hose, and fish-off-the-pier kind of girl. I'm loyal even when others are not.

I've wrestled with brothers, played Barbie with neighbors, and stayed up too late reading *just one more chapter.* I'm from **BIG** Sunday dinners, steaming hot tea, and Saturday morning coin-sized pancakes. I grew up with Tupperware, paper bag lunches, Yorkshire pudding, and mashed potatoes.

Lots of mashed potatoes.

My family is a finish-what-you-start, bargain shopping, home cooking, and respect-your-elders kind of family. I am one of four children framed in memories on a wall. I jumped off docks, endured eight-hour trips that took twelve, and sat in the middle bench seat of the family sedan.

I am a *wait until you enter the house before driving away* kind of mom. I boil the kettle in a crisis, and I know that a job worth doing is worth doing right.

I am a fixer of old things, painter of everything, cleansed and forgiven child of God. I believe that nothing matters more than the Lord Jesus Christ and who I believe He is.

From the Author

Dear Reader,

Your time is precious, and I count it a privilege that you chose to journey with Jessie and Rick through Fatal Homecoming. Often, the things I am studying in the bible make their way into my novels. At the time of writing Fatal Homecoming, I was reading the book of Joshua.

Joshua 4 describes the pile of stones the Israelites built as a memorial to God. Those stones were evidence of the Lord's provision for them. The memorial was a reminder to future generations that God had delivered his people.

In Fatal Homecoming, Jessie needed to remember God's provision. As I wrote her story, I made my own pile of stones. They gave words to my faith and helped me remember that God is a God of action.

I set a goal to gather 'one stone' each day for one year. One acknowledgment of God's goodness, His mercy, and His unchanging dependability affirmed that God hears and answers prayer.

I placed a jar on my kitchen windowsill to hold these reminders. They were a collection of answered prayers ready to remind the future generation that my God is good. These were proof of God's action, even if His answer to my request was no. They were more than words on paper, and they were more than a pile of rocks by a river. They were a reference point. They mark where God met me and gave me a story to share so that others may also know and believe.

My goal in writing is to glorify God. It is my prayer that Fatal Homecoming not only entertained you, but also stirred you to draw closer to the Father and trust His will for your life. I want to take this opportunity to encourage you to gather your own pile of stones and remember to believe that your God is good. Always.

Stacey

Other Romance and Suspense from WIP

Meet the Camerons.

Follow the Cameron family through each of the books and learn how these siblings fight together and sometimes even against each other.

Visit Amazing Grace, North Carolina

The Amazing Grace series is complete!

Four intensely satisfying stories of love and survival.

Thank you
for reading our books!

Look for other books
published by

Pursued Books
an imprint of

Write Integrity Press
www.WriteIntegrity.com

.

33059519R00194

Made in the USA
Middletown, DE
11 January 2019